GRANDMOTHER ELSIE

GRANDMOTHER ELSIE
A Sequel to Elsie's Widowhood

MARTHA FINLEY

The web of our life is of a mingled yarn,
good and ill together.

—SHAKESPEARE

FULL &
QUART
PRESS

An Imprint of
Holly Hall Publications

Grandmother Elsie
Book 8 of The Elsie Books

by Martha Finley

Any revisions or special features in this edition:
© 1998 Holly Hall Publications
ISBN 1-888306-41-6

Published by:
Holly Hall Publications
255 S. Bridge Street
P.O. Box 254
Elkton, MD 21922-0254

Send requests for information to the above address.

Cover illustration by Kathleen Taylor Kist

Printed in the United States of America.

CHAPTER 1

Every state,
Allotted to the race of man below,
Is in proportion, doom'd to taste some sorrow.

THE ION FAMILY WAS AT HOME AGAIN after their summer on the New Jersey coast.

It was a delightful morning early in October — the dewdrops on the still green grass of the neatly kept lawn sparkled in the rays of the newly risen sun. The bright waters of the lakelet also sparkled as, ruffled by the breeze, they broke gently on the prow of the pretty rowboat moored to the little wharf. And the gardens were gay with bright-hued flowers, the trees gorgeous in their autumnal dress.

But though doors and windows were open and the gardener and his assistants were at work on the grounds, there seemed a strange quiet about the place. When the men spoke to each other it was in subdued tones. There was no sound — as in other days — of little feet running hither and thither, or of childish prattle or laughter.

Two horses stood ready saddled and bridled before the principal entrance to the mansion. Mr. Horace Dinsmore was pacing the veranda to and fro with slow, meditative steps, while Bruno, crouching beside the door, followed his movements with wistful, questioning eyes, doubtless wondering what had become of his accustomed merry, romping playmates.

A light step came down the hall, and a lady in riding hat and habit stepped from the open doorway. She stooped for an instant to touch the dog's head caressingly with a "Poor Bruno, do you miss your playfellows?" Then she glided quickly toward Mr. Dinsmore, who received her with open arms and tenderest caress.

Then, holding her off and scrutinizing the sweet, fair face with keen, searching eyes, "You are looking better and brighter than I dared to hope, my darling," he said. "Did you get some sleep?"

"Yes, papa, thank you — several hours." And you? Did you rest well?"

"Yes, daughter. How are the children?"

"No worse, Arthur says. Perhaps a trifle better. He, Elsie and Mammy are with them now, and 'Mamma' can be spared for a short ride with her father," she said, smiling lovingly into the eyes that were gazing with the tenderest fatherly affection upon her.

"That is right. You need the air and exercise sorely. A few more days of such close confinement and assiduous nursing would, I very much fear, tell seriously upon your health."

He led her to the side of her steed and assisted her into the saddle as they spoke, then vaulted into his own with the agility of youth.

"But where are Vi and her brothers?" Elsie asked, sending an inquiring glance from side to side.

"I sent them on in advance. I wanted you quite to myself this once," he answered, as they turned and rode at a brisk canter down the avenue.

"And I shall enjoy having my dear father all to myself for once," she rejoined, with a touch of old time gaiety in look and tone. "Ah, papa, never a day passes, I think I might almost say never an hour, in which I do not thank God for sparing you tome. You have loved and cherished me so long and so tenderly."

"My own dear child!" he said in reply, "you and your love are among the greatest blessings of my life."

As they rode on side by side they talked of the youngest two of her children — Rose and Walter — both quite ill with measles. They also spoke of her sister's family, where also there was sickness among the little ones and whither Mrs. Dinsmore had gone to assist in the nursing of her grandchildren; of the recent death of Enna at Magnolia Hall, the home of her daughter Molly; and of the anxiety of the younger Elsie because of a much longer than usual silence on the part of her absent betrothed.

She greatly feared that some evil had befallen him and she had not been able to hide her distress from these two — the mother and grandfather who loved her so. She had made a most earnest, unselfish effort to conceal it from all, especially her mother, whose tender heart was ever ready to bleed for anyone's woe, and who had already griefs and anxieties enough of her own.

They spoke of her with tenderest compassion and affectionate pride in her loveliness of person and character, and her brave endurance of her trial.

Enna's death could hardly be felt as personal loss either. But they sympathized deeply in the grief of her old father, with whom her faults seemed to be buried in her grave, while he cherished a lively remembrance of all that had ever given him pleasure in her looks, words, or ways.

He was growing old and feeble, and felt this death of his youngest child, a very heavy blow.

"My poor old father! I fear we shall not have him with us for very much longer," Mr. Dinsmore remarked with emotion.

Elsie's eyes glistened with unshed tears. "Dear old grandpa!" she murmured. "But, dear papa, be comforted! He may live for years yet, and should it please God to take him, we know that our loss will be his infinite gain."

"Yes, would that we had the same assurance in regard to all his children and grandchildren."

Silence fell between them for some minutes.

Elsie knew that her father, when making that last remark, was thinking more particularly of his half-sister, Mrs. Conly, and her daughter, Virginia.

The two had gone to a fashionable watering place to spend the last fortnight of their summer's sojourn up north and ere it expired Virginia had contracted a hasty marriage with a man of reputed wealth, whom she met there for the first time.

The match was made with the full consent and approval of her mother — who, on rejoining the Dinsmores and Travillas, boasted much of "Virginia's brilliant position and prospects" — but without the knowledge of any other relative. No opportunity of making inquiries about the character or real circumstances of the stranger to whom she committed the happiness of her life was afforded by Virginia to grandfather, uncle, or brother.

Of late Mrs. Conly had ceased to boast of the match — scarcely mentioned Virginia's name. And Mr. Dinsmore had learned from Calhoun and Arthur that Virginia's letters were no longer shown to anyone and seemed to irritate and depress their mother so unmistakably that they feared more and more that there was something very much amiss with their sister. Yet, the mother steadily evaded all inquiries on the subject.

Mr. Dinsmore presently told all this to his daughter, adding that he very much feared Virginia had made an utter wreck of her earthly happiness.

"Poor Virgie!" sighed Elsie. "Ah, if only she had been blessed with such a father as mine!" turning upon him a look of grateful love.

"Or such a mother as my granddaughters have," added Mr. Dinsmore, smiling into the soft, sweet eyes.

"What blessings my darlings are! How good and lovable in spite of my failures in right training and example," she said in sincere humility.

"Those failures and mistakes have been very few, I think," was his reply. "You have tried very earnestly and prayerfully to train them up in the way they should go. And God is faithful to His promises — your children do not depart from the right way. They do arise and call you blessed."

"Papa," she said in moved tones, after a moment's silence, "We must not forget how much is due to the training, the example, and the prayers of their father."

"No, daughter, and we can always plead in their behalf the precious promises to the seed of the righteous. 'I will pour my Spirit upon the seed, and my blessings upon thine offspring.' 'A good man leaveth his inheritance to his children's children.'"

"Yes, father, how often have those promises been my comfort and support as the inheritance of both my children and myself — inherited by me from both you and my sainted mother and her pious ancestors."

"And from mine — for my mother was a devoted Christian and came from a long line of God-fearing men and women. But I see nothing yet of Edward and his party. They must have taken another road."

"Yes, sir, and shall we not turn now? I ought not to be long away from my poor sick darlings."

"I think it would be well to return by the other road. We shall reach it in a moment and our ride will be lengthened by but a half mile or so."

She acquiesced in his decision as was her custom.

On the homeward way, as they neared the crossroad leading to the city, they saw a boy on horseback coming at a hard gallop in their direction.

On catching sight of them he held aloft what looked like a letter, waving it about his head in evident desire to attract their attention. Then, as he reached their road, he halted and waited for them to come up.

"Mr. Dinsmore, from the Oaks or Ion, isn't it?" he queried, lifting his cap and bowing to the lady and her escort as they reined in their steeds close at hand.

"Yes."

"A telegram for you, sir."

Mr. Dinsmore took the missive, tore it open and glanced at the contents; then, handing it to Elsie, paid the boy and dismissed him.

"Oh, my poor darling!" she exclaimed, her tears dropping upon the paper. "Father, what shall we do? Tell her at once? Perhaps that would be best."

"Yes, I think it is her right. But, of course, it must be done as gently as possible. Dear daughter, do not grieve too sorely for her. Try to trust her as well as yourself in your heavenly Father's hands."

"I will, papa, I will! But, oh, my heart bleeds for her!"

"Will you break the news to her? Or shall I?"

"My kindest of fathers! You would, if possible, spare me every trial, bear all my burdens. But perhaps the dear child may suffer less in hearing the sad news from her mother's lips, as, in her place, I could bear it better from yours than from any other."

"Unselfish as ever, my darling," he said. "But I believe you are right — that the blow will be somewhat softened to Elsie coming to her through the medium of her tender and dearly loved mother."

"I think, papa," Mrs. Travilla said, checking her horse to a walk as they entered the avenue at Ion, "I shall reserve my communication until my poor child has had her breakfast."

He expressed approval of her decision, adding interrogatively, "You will breakfast with the family this morning?"

"Yes, sir, if I find all going well in the sick room."

A servant was in waiting to lead the horses away to the stable. Violet, Edward, Harold and Herbert just returned from their ride, were on the veranda.

Edward hastened to assist his mother to alight and all gathered about her and their grandfather with morning greetings spoken in cheerful but subdued tones. No one forgetting for a moment the illness of the little brother and sister, but all inquiring anxiously how they and "Mamma" had passed the night and what was Cousin Arthur's report of their condition this morning.

"No worse, my dears. And we will hope that they may soon be decidedly better," the mother answered, returning their greetings with affectionate warmth and smiling sweetly upon them. "But you must let me go at once to the sick room, and if all is well, I shall be down presently to breakfast with grandpa and you."

That announcement was heard with greater pleasure

because her loved face had seldom been seen at the table for some days past.

Her face was bright and hopeful as she spoke, but an unusual expression of sadness and anxiety came over it as she turned quickly away and went swiftly through the spacious entrance hall and up the broad stairway. No earthly eye saw that look, but the traces of tears on her mother's cheeks had not escaped Vi's keen observation.

"Grandpa," she said in low, tremulous tones, following him into the library, whither he went to await the summons to breakfast, "What has been distressing mamma so? Is it that she is so anxious about Rosie and Walter? May I not know?"

Mr. Dinsmore paused a moment before he replied. "You shall know all about it, my dear child, before very long. Be satisfied for the present with the assurance that your mother's distress is for another's woe. You know what a tender, sympathetic heart she has. I cannot deny that our little ones are seriously ill, but their case is very far from hopeless."

CHAPTER 11

Within her heart was his image,
Cloth'd in the beauty of love and youth,
as last she beheld him,
Only more beautiful made by his
deathlike silence and absence.

—LONGFELLOW

THE SICK ONES WERE SLEEPING QUIETLY when the mother entered. The doctor had already breakfasted and would assist Aunt Chloe and Dinah in watching beside them for the next hour, so the two Elsies — mother and daughter — went down together to the breakfast parlor.

They were a more silent party than usual at mealtime, for no one could forget the two absent members of the family, or that they were suffering upon beds of sickness. Yet, there was no gloom in any face or voice. Their few words were spoken in cheerful tones, and each seemed unselfishly intent upon promoting the comfort and happiness of all the others — on the part of the children, especially their grandfather and mother; each young heart was evidently full to overflowing of tenderest sympathy and love for her.

She had been closely confined to the sick room for several days, so that it was a treat to have her with them at breakfast and at family worship, which followed directly upon the conclusion of the meal.

It surprised them a little that when the short service came to an end, she did not even then return at once to her sick little ones. But putting on a garden hat invited her eldest daughter to do likewise and come with her for a short stroll in the grounds.

"It will do us both good," she said as they stepped from the veranda upon the broad, graveled walk. "The air is so sweet and pure at this early hour, and you have not been out in it at all, have you?"

"No, mamma, and what a treat it is to take it in your dear company," Elsie responded, gathering a lovely, sweet-scented flower and placing it in the bosom of her mother's dress.

"Thank you, love," Mrs. Travilla said; then, went on to speak feelingly about the beauty and fragrance that surrounded and the unnumbered blessings of their lot in life.

"Mamma, you seem to have a heart always filled with love and gratitude to God and never to be troubled with the least rebellious feeling, or any doubts or fears for the future," remarked Elsie, sighing slightly as she spoke.

"Have you any right or reason to indulge repining, doubts, or fears when we know that all is ordered for us by One who loves us with an everlasting and infinite love, and who is all-wise and all-powerful? Oh, darling, no! Well may we say with the Psalmist, 'I will fear no evil, for thou art with me; thy rod and thy staff they comfort me. Surely goodness and mercy shall follow me all the days of my life; and I will dwell in the house of the Lord forever.' Oh, what a blessed assurance! Goodness and mercy while here in this world of trial — all things working together for our good, that so we may be brought at last safely to our desired haven — and then to be forever with the Lord."

"Mamma, I have been so anxious and troubled about my little brother and sister, and about Lester. I needed the lesson you have just given me and I hope I shall profit by it."

"My dearest child, have faith in God. Try to believe with all your heart that he will never send you or any of his children one unneeded pang. I am sure you could never think I — your tender mother — would give you the slightest pain except for your certain good. And what is my love for you compared to that of your Savior who died that you might live!"

"Mamma," cried the young girl, pausing in her walk, laying her hand on her mother's arm and looking searchingly into the sweet, compassionate face, while her own grew deathly pale. "What is it you are trying to prepare me for? Oh, mamma!"

A rustic seat stood close at hand.

"Let us sit down here for a moment, dear daughter," Mrs. Travilla said, drawing Elsie to it with an arm about her waist. "You are right, my child — I have news for you. Oh, not the worst, dearest!" as Elsie seemed to gasp for breath. "Lester lives, but is very ill with typhoid fever."

"Mamma!" cried Elsie, starting to her feet, "I must go to him! I must go at once! Oh, dearest mother, do not hinder me!" and she clasped her hands in piteous entreaty, the big tears rapidly chasing each other down her pale cheeks.

"If I could go with you," faltered the mother, "or your grandfather. But I can neither leave nor take my little ones, and he would not consent to leave me, or his poor old father, who seems just tottering on the verge of the grave."

"I know! I see it! But, oh, mother, mother! How can I let him die alone in a strange land? Think if it had been you and my father!"

"What is your entreaty, daughter?" Mr. Dinsmore asked, coming up and laying his hand affectionately upon his grandchild's shoulder.

"To go to him — to Lester, grandpa. Oh, how can I stay away and leave him to die alone? To die for lack of the good nursing I could give him, perhaps to the saving of his life!"

"My poor child! My poor child!" he said, caressing her. "We will see what can be done in the way of finding a suitable escort, and if that can be obtained your mother will not, I think, withhold her consent."

He had been telling the news to the others and Edward had followed him, anxious to express the sympathy for his sister with which his heart was full.

"An escort, grandpa?" he said. "Would mine be sufficient? Mamma, if you will permit me, I shall gladly go to Lester, either with or without Elsie."

"My dear boy!" was all his mother said, her tones tremulous with emotion, while his grandfather turned and regarded him with doubtful scrutiny.

"Oh, thank you, brother!" cried Elsie. "Mamma, surely you can trust me to him! Who loves me better? Except yourself — and who would take such tender care of me?"

"Mamma, I would guard her with my life!" exclaimed Edward earnestly.

"My dear son, I do not doubt it," Mrs. Travilla answered, turning upon her father a half-inquiring, half-entreating look.

"If no older or more experienced person can be found."

He paused, and Elsie burst out, "Oh, grandfather, dear grandpa, don't say that! There is no time to lose! No time to look for another escort!"

"That is true, my child, and we will not waste any time. Make your preparations as rapidly as you can, and if nothing better offers in the meanwhile, and your mother consents to Edward's proposition, you shall go with him — and Ben who traveled all over Europe with your father and myself — as your protectors."

She thanked him fervently through her tears, while her mother said, "Ah, yes, that is a good thought, papa! Ben shall go with them."

"Better go now and at once select whatever you wish to take with you, and set someone to packing your trunks," he said. "Edward, you do likewise, and I will examine the morning papers for information in regard to trains and the sailing of the next steamer. Daughter, dear," to Mrs. Travilla, "you need give yourself no concern about any of these matters."

"No, I shall trust everything to you, my best of fathers, and go back at once to my sick darlings," she said, giving him a look of grateful love.

Then passing her arm affectionately about her

daughter's waist, she drew her on toward the house, her father and son accompanying them.

She parted with Elsie at the door of the sickroom, embracing her tenderly and bidding her " 'Be strong and of a good courage, my darling, for 'the eternal God is they refuge, and underneath are the everlasting arms.' "

"Dearest mamma, what sweet words!" said the weeping girl. "Oh, how glad I am that God reigns! And that I know He will send to each of His children just what is best."

She turned away as the door closed upon her mother and found Vi close at her side.

There was a silent affectionate embrace and with their arms about each other, they sought Elsie's dressing room.

"Grandpa and Edward have told me," Violet said, "and you will let me help you, my poor dear sister? Help in thinking and selecting what you will want to carry with you."

"Gladly, thankfully, for, oh, I seem scarcely able to collect my thoughts! How can I leave mamma and all of you? And the darling little brother and sister so ill? And yet, how can I stay away from Lester when he is sick and alone in a strange land, with not a friend to speak a cheering word, smooth his pillow, give his medicine, or see that he has proper food? Oh, Vi, can I help going to him? Even at the sacrifice of leaving all other near and dear ones?"

"I think mother would have done it for papa," Violet answered, kissing Elsie's cheek.

Mr. Dinsmore, having first seen Ben, and found him more than willing to go with the children of the master he had loved as his own soul, went to the library. He looked over the papers, and had just found the information he sought, when the sound of horses' hoofs on the avenue drew his attention, and glancing from the window he saw the Roselands carriage drive up with his sister, Mrs. Conley, inside.

He hastened out to assist her to alight.

"Good morning, Horace," she said. "Is my son Arthur here?"

"Yes, Louise, he has spent the last hour or more in attendance upon our sick little ones. Ah, here he is to speak for himself!" as the young doctor stepped from the open doorway. "But won't you come in?"

She demurred. "Is there any danger, Arthur?"

"Danger of what, mother?"

"You certainly understood me," she said half angrily, "danger of contagion, of course."

"None for you, surely, mother, and none you could carry home unless you came in personal contact with the sick children."

"I shall sit here for a moment, then," she said, stepping from the carriage and taking a chair upon the veranda. "How are they today?"

"The sick little ones? The disease has not yet reached its crisis."

"I hope they'll get safely over it. It's a good thing to have over. How soon can you be spared from here, Arthur?"

"Now, mother, if I am needed elsewhere, I shall not be needed here — at least am not likely to be — for some hours."

"Then I wish you'd come home directly to see what you can do for your grandfather. He doesn't seem at all well today."

"My father ill?" Mr. Dinsmore exclaimed in a tone of alarm and concern.

"It hardly amounts to that, I presume," Mrs. Conly answered coldly, "but he is not well — didn't eat a mouthful of breakfast."

"Grandpa, did you find what you wanted in the morning paper?" queried Edward, joining them at that moment. "Ah, Aunt Louise, how do you do?"

She nodded indifferently, listening with some curiosity for her brother's reply.

"Yes," he said. "And I think you should leave tonight. For by so doing you will reach New York in time to take the next steamer, if you meet with no great detention on the way. Do you think you can both be ready?"

"I certainly can, sir, and I have no doubt Elsie will also."

"What is it? Off to Europe?" asked Mrs. Conly in surprise. "What could call you two children there at this time?"

Mr. Dinsmore briefly stated the facts, giving the news of the morning, Elsie's wish, and Edward's offer to be her escort to Italy.

"If she were a daughter of mine, I should consider a female companion an absolute necessity," was Mrs. Conly's comment.

"She will take her maid of course," said Mr. Dinsmore and Edward, both speaking at once.

"Pooh! A maid! I mean a lady relative or friend. I said a companion, and that a maid could not be."

"I should be extremely glad if such could be found in the few hours that we have for our preparations," said her brother, "but I know of none. The Fairview family are absent, Violet is too young —."

"Of course," interrupted Mrs. Conly, "but there are other relatives. I would go myself if my means would warrant the expense."

"If you are in earnest, Louise, you need not hesitate for a moment on that score. It shall not cost you a penny," her brother said, looking at her in pleased but half-incredulous surprise.

"I was never more earnest," she answered. "I don't think you give me much credit for affection for your grandchildren, yet I certainly care too much for the one in question to willingly see her undertake such a journey without the support of female companionship. And I can be spared from home if you and Arthur will look after father. I have no young child now, and Aunt Marcia is fully capable of taking charge of household matters. If you wish me to go you have only to say so and guarantee my expenses. I shall go home, oversee the packing of my trunks and be ready as soon as the young people are."

"Your offer is a most kind one, Louise, and I accept it even without waiting to consult with my daughter," Mr. Dinsmore said.

"Then I must go home at once, and see about my preparations immediately," she said, rising to take her leave.

Arthur Conly as well as Edward Travilla had been silent listeners to the short dialogue.

"Can you spare your mother, Arthur?" his uncle asked.

"We must sir, if it please her to go, and for the sake of my two sweet cousins — Elsie senior and Elsie junior — I willingly consent. You take the night train, I understand?" turning to Edward.

"Yes, tonight."

"I shall see that my mother is at the depot on time," and with that they took their departure, Mr. Dinsmore saying, as he bid them adieu, that he should ride over presently to see his father.

Turning toward Edward, he saw that the lad's eyes were following the Roselands carriage down the avenue, his face wearing a rueful look.

"Grandpa," he said, with a sigh, "I see no necessity for Aunt Louise's company, and, indeed, should very much prefer to be without it."

"You forget that you are speaking to your grandfather of his sister?" Mr. Dinsmore answered with a touch of sternness in his tone.

"I beg your pardon, sir," returned Edward. "She is so unlike you that I am apt to forget the relationship."

"I know you do not always find you aunt's company agreeable," remarked Mr. Dinsmore, "and I do not blame you on that account. Yet I do think it will be an advantage to you, and especially your sister, to have with you a woman of her age, and knowledge of the world. I wish I could go with you myself, but I cannot think of leaving either my old father or your mother in this time of trial."

"No, sir, oh no!" Delightful as it would be to both of us for you to make one of our little party, we would not for the world deprive dear mamma of the support and comfort of your presence here; nor our dear old grandfather either."

CHAPTER III

Filial ingratitude!
Is it not as this mouth should tear this hand
For lifting food to 't?

—SHAKESPEARE, KING LEAR

"THIS IS A VERY SUDDEN resolve of yours, mother, isn't it?" Dr. Conly asked, as they drove through the great gates at Ion into the highway.

"It is, Arthur, for I had not dreamed of such a wild scheme on the part of those two silly children until I heard of it from their grandfather's lips. Nor could I have believed he would sanction such folly. They ought to make Elsie stay where she is and if young Leland dies, it will rid the family of a prospective plebian alliance."

"Very possibly of the sweet girl also," was Arthur's grave response.

"Nonsense! It is only in novels that girls die of broken hearts."

"Granting that for argument's sake, it must be very hard to live with one."

"Well, it seems she is to be allowed to go, and my offer removes the most serious objection. Yet, I have no idea the sacrifice on my part will be at all appreciated."

"Then why make it, mother? I can readily find a substitute. There is Mrs. Foster, whose health would be greatly benefited by a long sea voyage. She, I feel certain, would think it a great boon to be allowed this opportunity of going without expense in the company of two young people of whom she is very fond. And you know, mother, that though poor now, she was formerly wealthy, is a perfect lady, and her having been in Europe once or twice would make her all the more valuable a companion to them."

"You are quite too late with your suggestion, Arthur," was the coldly spoken reply. "I have given my word and shall not break it."

Her son gave her a look of keen scrutiny, then turned his face from her with a scarcely audible sigh. He read her motives and feelings far more clearly than she suspected.

The truth was she was weary of the dullness of home now that the shadow of bereavement was upon it. The etiquette of mourning forbade her attendance at public assemblages of whatever kind, except church, and did not allow even so much as a formal call upon strangers or acquaintances. The society of her now old, feeble, and depressed father was wearisome to her also.

Besides, she long had a hankering after a European tour and this was too good an opportunity to let slip. Also, it would give her a chance to see for herself what was the trouble with Virginia, whose letters of late had been of a very disquieting kind — full of reproaches and vague hints of unhappiness and disappointment in her new life.

There would probably be a few hours between their arrival in New York and the sailing of the steamer, in which she could call to see Virginia and learn with certainty exactly how she was situated.

Mrs. Travilla received the news of her aunt's offer with a gratitude that it by no means merited. And the young Elsie, though not fond of her Aunt Louise's society, felt that her presence might prove a comfort and support when she and Edward should find themselves strangers in a foreign land.

The mother sought this dear eldest child with loving words of cheer and counsel whenever she could be spared from the sick-room, and Violet, Harold and Herbert hung about her as a treasure soon to be snatched from them, eager to render any assistance in his or her power.

The hour of parting came all too soon, and with many tears and embraces, the young travelers were sent on their way.

The mother's last words to Elsie, as she held her close

to her heart with many a tear and tender caress, were "'Be strong and of a good courage, fear not, nor be afraid of them, for the Lord thy God, He will not fail thee, nor forsake thee.' To Him, the God of your fathers, do I trust you, my precious child."

"You also, my dear, dear boy!" taking Edward's hand. "But rejoice in the thought that you are together, mutual helpers and comforters."

"Be sure to telegraph us from New York, Edward, again as soon as possible after landing on the other side, and a third time when you have seen Lester and can report his exact condition," was Mr. Dinsmore's parting injunction, as with a most affectionate farewell he left them in the sleeping car.

Mrs. Conly had joined them at the depot, according to promise.

All three retired at once to their berths, and Elsie wept herself to sleep, thinking of the dear ones left behind — especially the mother who had so tenderly cherished her from her birth and the sick little ones who, she feared, might not be there to welcome her return. Thinking too of him to whom she was going, his probable suffering, and the dread possibility that at her journey's end she should find only his grave.

They reached New York in good season, having met with no accident or detention. The steamer would not leave for some hours, but it was Elsie's desire to go directly on board.

"I think that will be your best plan," said Mrs. Conly. "You can then settle yourself in your state room at once. And while Dinah unpacks what you will need on the voyage, you can lie in your berth and rest. You are looking greatly fatigued."

"You will come with us, Aunt Louise, will you not?" both the young people asked.

"No, I must see Virginia. I shall have time for an hour's chat with her and yet reach the vessel some time before the hour fixed for her sailing. Edward, will you see that my luggage is taken aboard?"

"Certainly, aunt, but shall we not first drive to Virginia's residence and leave you there? And I will return for you after seeing my sister and the luggage is taken on board the steamer."

"No, not at all!" she answered stiffly. "I am obliged for your offer, but where would be the use? You may tell Ben to call a hack for me. I'll have it wait at Virginia's door and drive me to the wharf when I am ready to go."

Edward, thinking he had never known her so considerate and kind, hastened to carry out her wishes, bidding Ben engage two hacks — one for Mrs. Conly and another for themselves.

Consideration for her nephew and niece had nothing to do with Mrs. Conly's plans and arrangements. If, as she greatly feared, Virginia were living in other than aristocratic style, she would not for the world have it known among the relatives who had heard her boasts in regard to Virgie's grand match — "so much better than Isa had been led into while under the care of her grandfather and uncle."

She had never before heard of the street mentioned in Virginia's last letter, and she had misgivings as to its being one of the more fashionable for the abodes of the wealthy. The curiously scrutinizing look and odd smile of the hack driver when she gave him the address did not tend to reassure her.

"Drive me there as quickly as you can," she ordered, drawing herself up and flashing an indignant glance at him. "I have no time to waste."

"Sure, mum, I'll do that same," he returned, touching his horse with the whip.

"Where are you taking me? What do you mean bringing me into such a vile region as this?" she demanded presently, as the hack turned into a narrow and very dirty street.

"It's the shortest cut to the place ye said ye wanted to go to, mum," he answered shortly.

She sank back with a sigh and closed her eyes for the

moment. She was very weary with her long journey and more depressed than she had ever been in her life before.

The drive seemed the longest and most unpleasant she had ever undertaken. She began to wish she had been content to sail for Europe without trying to find Virginia. But at last the vehicle stopped, the driver reached down from his seat and opened the door.

His passenger put out her head, glanced this way and that, scanned the house before her and angrily demanded, "What are you stopping here for?"

"Bekase ye tould me to, mum. It's the place ye said ye wanted to come to."

Mrs. Conly looked at the number over the door, saw that it was the one she had given him. Then in a voice she vainly tried to make coldly indifferent, inquired of some children who had gathered on the sidewalk to gaze in open-mouthed curiosity at her and the hack, if this were —— street.

The answer confirmed the driver's assertion and she hastily alighted.

The house was a large tenement swarming with inhabitants, as was evidenced by the number of heads in nearly every front window, drawn thither by the unusual event of the stopping of a hack before the door of entrance. It stood wide open, giving a view of an unfurnished hall and stairway, both of which were in a very untidy condition.

"Does Henry Neuville live here?" Mrs. Conly asked, addressing the group of staring children.

"Dunno," said one. "Guess not," said another.

"Mebbe them the grand folks as moved into the second story front t'other week," observed a third. "I'll show ye the way, lady." And he rushed past her into the house and ran nimbly up the dirty stairs.

Mrs. Conly lifted her skirts and followed, her heart sinking like lead. Could it be possible that Virginia had come to this?

Halting before the door of the front room on the second floor, the lad gave a thundering rap, then opened it, shouting, "Here's a old lady to see ye, Mrs. Novel, if that's yer name."

"What do you mean by rushing in on me in this rude way, you young rascal?" demanded a shrill female voice, which Mrs. Conly instantly recognized as that of her daughter. "Begone instantly! Begone, I say!"

"Go, go!" Mrs. Conley said to the boy, in half smothered tones, putting a small coin into his hand. Then staggering into the room she dropped into a chair, gasping for breath.

"Virginia, Virginia! Can it be possible that I find you in such a place as this?" she cried, as the latter started up from a lounge on which she had been lying with a paper-covered novel in her hand.

Her hair was in crimping pins, her dress most slovenly, and her surroundings were in keeping with her personal appearance.

"Mamma!" she exclaimed in utter astonishment and confusion. "How did you get here? How did you come? You should have sent me word. I have no way to accommodate you."

"Don't be alarmed, I have no intention of staying more than an hour. I start for Europe by today's steamer with Elsie and Edward Travilla. Lester Leland's ill, dying I presume, and the silly love-sick girl must needs rush to the rescue."

"And why are you to go with her?" Why don't the mother and grandfather and the whole family accompany her — after their usual fashion of all keeping together?"

"Because Rosie and Walter are down with measles — much too ill to travel."

"And you are going to Europe to enjoy yourself, while I must live here in a New York tenement house occupied by the dregs of society as the wife of a drunkard, gambler and rake. He's a man — or rather a brut — who lives by his wits. He abuses me like the pickpocket that he is, half starves me, and expects me to do all the work — cooking, cleaning, and everything else, even to washing and ironing of the few clothes he hasn't pawned. Me!

A lady brought up to have servants to wait upon her at every turn!"

"Oh, Virgie, Virgie! It can't be so bad as that!" cried her mother, clasping her hands in an agony of distress, and gazing piteously at her, the hot tears running down her face.

"I tell you it is that and worse! And it's all your fault for you made the match! You hurried me into it lest grandpa, uncle or brothers should interfere — find out that the man's morals were not good according to their high standard, and prevent me from marrying him."

"You were in as great haste and as much opposed to their interference as I, Virginia!" the mother retorted, drawing herself up in proud anger.

"Well, and what of that? You brought me up, and I was only following out the teachings you have given me from the cradle. I tell you it was your doing. But I must reap what you have sowed. I wish I were dead!" She flung her book at her as she spoke, turned and paced the room, her hands clenched, her eyes flashing, her teeth set hard.

She had not drawn near her mother, or given her one word of welcome or thanks for having turned aside from her journey to inquire into her welfare.

"'Oh, sharper than a serpent's tooth it is to have a thankless child!'" exclaimed Mrs. Conly in anguished accents, rising as if to go, but instantly falling heavily to the floor.

Virginia rushed to her side, half-frantic with terror.

"Oh, mother, mother, what have I done! I know you are the best friend I have in the world!" she cried, stooping over her, loosening her bonnet strings and dress and trying vainly to lift her to the lounge. She was a large, heavy woman and now in this state of utter insensibility — her face purple, her breathing hoarse.

The sound of her fall and Virginia's terrified shriek had brought the neighbors flocking upon the scene, some of the boldest opening the door and ushering themselves in without the ceremony of knocking.

"The lady's in a fit!" cried a woman, hurrying to Virginia's assistance. "You've druv her to distraction.

You shouldn't a been so abusive. I could hear ye clear into my room a scoldin' and accusin' of her makin' your match fer ye."

"Run for the doctor, some of you!" cried Virginia, standing by the couch where, with the woman's help, she had laid her mother, wringing her hands in helpless distress. "Oh, she'll die! She'll die! Mother, mother! I'm sorry I was so cruel! Oh, I take it all back. Oh, mother, speak to me!"

"'Tain't no use," said the woman, "she don't hear ye. An' if she did she couldn't speak. I've seen folks struck with apoplexy before."

"Oh, will she die? Will she die?" groaned the wretched daughter, dropping on her knees beside the couch.

"Can't tell, mum. Sometimes they die in a little bit, and sometimes they git purty well over it and live on for years. Here, let me put another pillar under her head and some o' ye there run and fetch the coldest water that ever ye can git."

Someone had summoned a physician and he presently came hurrying in. His first act was to send everyone from the room except the patient and her two attendants.

With tears and sobs Virginia besought him to save her mother's life.

"I shall certainly do my best, madam," he said, "but very little can be done at the present. What was the immediate cause of the attack?"

Virginia answered vaguely that her mother was fatigued with a long journey had been worried and fretted.

"This is not her home?" he asked, glancing around the meanly furnished dirty room.

"No, neither she nor I have been accustomed to such surroundings," answered Virginia haughtily. "Can you not see that we are ladies? We are from the south, and mother has but just arrived. Oh, tell me, is she going to die?"

"Her recovery is doubtful. If she has other near relatives who care to see her alive, I advise you summon them with all speed."

"Oh, dear! Oh, dear! I must save her!" cried Virginia

frantically wringing her hands. "I can't have her die. They'll say I killed her! But every word I said was true. She did all in her power to make the match that has ruined my happiness and my prospects for life."

"So you, her own daughter, has brought this on by cruel taunts and reproaches?" the physician said in a tone of mingled contempt and indignation. "I hope you feel that the least you can do now is to take the best possible care of her."

"How can I?" sobbed Virginia. "I've no money to pay a nurse or buy comforts for mother, and I know nothing about nursing or cooking for sick or well. I wasn't brought up to work."

A boy now came to the door with a message from the hackman. He couldn't stay any longer if the lady wasn't going to the steamer, and he wanted his pay.

Virginia opened a small satchel that had dropped from her mother's hand. She found her purse, paid the man his dues, and counting the remainder told the doctor there was enough to provide what would be needed for the patient until some relatives could be summoned, and that should be done at once by telegrams to be paid by the recipients.

The doctor approved, and kindly offered to attend to sending the messages for her.

CHAPTER IV

O gloriously upon the deep
The gallant vessel rides,
And she is mistress of the winds,
And mistress of the tides.

—MISS LANDO

MEANWHILE EDWARD had taken his sister on board the steamer, and she, greatly exhausted by grief, anxiety, and fatigue, had at once retired to her berth.

Edward also was weary and in need of sleep, so presently went to his stateroom, leaving Ben to attend to the luggage and watch for Mrs. Conly's arrival.

Faithful Ben waited patiently for a couple of hours, then began to grow uneasy lest Mrs. Conly should not arrive in time. Another hour passed, and he reluctantly roused his young master to ask what could be done?

"What's wanted?" Edward asked, waked by Ben's loud rap on the state room door.

"Miss Louise she hasn't come yet, Marse Ed'ard," he said, "and de steamah'll be startin' fo' long. I don't know whar to go to look her up, so please excuse me for rousin' ye, sah."

"Hasn't come yet, do you say, Ben? And the vessel is about to sail?" exclaimed Edward in dismay, springing from his berth to open the door. "Why, yes," looking at his watch, "there's barely half an hour left, and I don't see what we can do."

"No time now fo' me to go an' hunt up Miss Louise, Marse Ed'ard. I'se berry sorry, sah, dat I didn't come soonah to ax you 'bout it, but I didn't like to 'sturb you," said Ben, looking much distressed.

"Never mind, Ben," Edward answered kindly, "you couldn't have gone for her, because she gave me no address, and I have not the least idea where to send for her."   "Den what am to be done, sah?"

"We will have to sail without her. I could not ask my sister to wait for the next steamer," Edward said, more as if thinking aloud than talking to Ben.

The latter bowed respectfully and withdrew, but only to come hurrying back the next moment with a telegram from Virginia.

"Mother taken suddenly ill. Remains with me. Send luggage to No. – – Street.

This news of his aunt's illness caused Edward regret not wholly unmingled with satisfaction in the thought of being spared her companionship on the voyage and afterward.

He read the message aloud to Ben. "You see it would have done no good if we could have gone for her," he remarked. "But go, make haste to have the baggage sent ashore to the address given here."

Elsie's stateroom adjoined her brother's. She, too, had been roused by Ben's knock and overheard part of what passed between him and his young master. Dinah also was listening.

"What dat dey say, Miss Elsie?" she queried in a startled tone. "Miss Louise sick?"

"I think that was what Master Edward said, but go to his door, Dinah, and ask."

Edward came himself with his answer and bringing a second telegram — this time from their grandfather saying the children were decidedly better, all the rest of the family well.

"Oh, what good news!" exclaimed Elsie. "But poor Aunt Louise! I wish we knew her exact condition. Do you not think it must have been a sudden seizure?"

"Yes, of either illness or desire to remain behind. Don't let it worry you, sister dear. You have already quite enough anxiety to endure."

"No," she said with a sweet, patient smile, "I am trying

not to be anxious or troubled about anything, but to obey the sweet command, 'casting all your care upon Him.'"

"'For He careth for you,'"added Edward, completing the quotation. "It is, as you say, a sweet command, most restful to those who obey it. Have you slept?"

"Yes, I have had a long and refreshing nap. Still, I have not recovered from my fatigue, and shall not leave my stateroom for some time yet."

"Let me send in your supper," he said. "I hope it will refresh you still more, and that after it you may feel equal to a turn on the deck with me. It will be moonlight, and if you wrap up well you will not find the air more than bracingly keen."

"Thank you," she said. "It is altogether likely I shall find exercise of a short promenade rather restful than otherwise, after being so long cramped up in the cars. You are a dear, good brother to me, Ned," she added, laying her hand affectionately on his arm as he sat on the edge of the berth close by her side. "But how strange it seems that we two are starting off on this long voyage alone!"

"I'm so proud to be trusted to take care of you, Elsie," he returned, bending over her and tenderly smoothing her luxuriant hair. "I used to look up to you years ago, but now —."

"You look down on me?" she interrupted sportively. "No great fear, Master Ned, while I lie here."

"Nor when we stand side by side," he returned in the same tone, "seeing I have grown to be a full head taller than you. But truth compels me to acknowledge that I am your superior in nothing else except physical strength."

"You might add knowledge of the world. You have had to rely on your own judgment so much oftener than I who have so seldom left mamma's side. Dear, dear mamma! Oh, Ned, how long will it be before I see her again?"

She wept as she spoke and Edward felt, for the moment, strongly inclined to join her. But instead, he tried to cheer her.

"We will hope Cousin Arthur may prescribe a sea

voyage for grandpa and the children before long, and then we shall have the whole family joining us in Italy."

"How delightful that would be, Ned!" she said, smiling through her tears.

"And do you know," he went on gaily, "it is strongly impressed upon me that we shall find Lester convalescent, and by good nursing and our cheering companionship so help it on that we shall have him a well man in a few weeks."

"Ah, if it might be so!" she sighed. "But He doeth all things well,' and oh how precious are His promises! 'As thy days thy strength shall be.' 'I will never leave thee nor forsake thee.' 'When thou passest through the waters, I will be with thee; and through the rivers, they shall not overflow thee: when thou walkest through the fire, thou shalt not be burned; neither shall the flames kindle upon thee.' And then that glorious assurance, 'We know that all things work together for good to them that love God.' Oh, Ned, our one great need is more and stronger faith!"

"Yes, the faith which worketh by love! Let me read you the eighth chapter of Romans. I do not know what could be more comforting," he said, taking a small Testament from his pocket.

"Thank you," she said when he had finished. "Ah, what could be sweeter than those concluding verses? 'For I am persuaded that neither death, nor life, nor angels, nor principalities, nor powers, nor things present, nor things to come, nor height, nor depth, nor any other creature, shall be able to separate us from the love of God which is in Christ Jesus our Lord!' "

"Elsie, I think if our mother had never done anything else for her children," remarked Edward earnestly, "they would owe her an eternal debt of gratitude for storing their minds with the very words of inspiration."

"Yes, 'the entrance of Thy words giveth light, it giveth understanding to the simple.' 'The law of Thy mouth is better unto me than thousands of gold and silver.' "

Ben came to the door. "Dey says dey's goin' to fetch

up de anchor and start de vessel, Marse Ed'ard. Don't you and Miss Elsie want for to see it?"

"Yes, sister, do you not wish to see the last you may, for the present, of your dear native land?" queried Edward in a lively tone. "'Twill take but a moment to don hat and shawl, and I shall be proud to give you the support of my arm."

"Yes, I do," she said, rising with alacrity and hastily making the needful preparations.

Ben preceded them to the deck and found comfortable seats for them in the front rank of those who were there on the same errand.

Elsie's tears began to flow as she saw the shore receding.

"Oh," she murmured very low and sadly, leaning on her brother's shoulder and clinging more closely to him, "shall we ever return? Shall we ever see again the dear land of our birth and all our loved ones left behind?"

"There is every reason to hope so, dear sister," he whispered in return. "A voyage to Europe is not the great and perilous undertaking it used to be, and we are under the same protecting care here as on land. 'And the Lord, He it is that doth go before thee, He will be with thee, He will not fail thee, neither forsake thee: fear not, neither be dismayed.'"

She looked her thanks. "'Fear not.' What a sweet command! I must, I will obey it. Oh, how true it is that in keeping His commandments there is great reward! I am fully convinced that in the perfect keeping of them all perfect happiness would be found."

A gentleman standing near turned suddenly round. The tones of Elsie's voice had reached him, though very few of the words.

"Ah, I thought I could not be mistaken in that voice," he said delightedly, and offered his hand in cordial greeting. "How are you, Miss Elsie? And you, Ned? Really you are the last people I expected to meet here, though the very ones I should prefer above all others as compagnons de voyage."

It was Philip Ross, Jr.

Neither of those addressed had ever enjoyed his society, and they were too sincere and true to reciprocate his expressions of gratification at the unexpected meeting. They accepted his offered hand, made kind inquiries in regard to his health and that of the other members of the family, and asked if any of them were on board.

"No," he said, "it's merely a business trip that I take quite frequently. But ma and the girls are in Paris now, went last June and expect to stay for another six months or longer. You two aren't here alone, eh?"

"Yes," Edward said.

"You don't say so!" cried Philip, elevating his eyebrows. "Who'd ever have believed your careful mother — not to speak of your grandfather — would ever trust you so far from home by yourselves!"

"Mr. Ross," Edward said, reddening, "I shall reach my majority a few months hence, and have been considered worthy of trust by both my mother and grandpa for years past."

"Mamma did not show the slightest hesitation in committing me to his care," added Elsie in her sweet, gentle tones.

"Glad to hear it! I didn't mean to insinuate that I didn't consider you worthy of all trust, Ned. I only thought that Mrs. Travilla and the old governor have always been so awfully strict and particular."

Elsie, to whom the slang term was new, looked at the speaker with a slightly puzzled expression. But Edward, who fully understood it, drew himself up with offended dignity.

"Permit me to remark, Mr. Ross, that so disrespectful an allusion to my honored grandfather can never be other that extremely offensive to me, and to all his children and grandchildren."

"Beg your pardon, Ned, and yours, Miss Elsie" (he would have liked to drop the Miss, but something in her manner prevented him). "I call my own father the governor — behind his back, you know — and meant no offense in applying the term to Mr. Dinsmore.

His apology was accepted and the talk turned upon the various objects of interest within sight as they passed through the harbor.

When there was little more to see but sky and water, Elsie retired to her stateroom, where she stayed until evening. Then Edward came for her and they passed an hour very enjoyably in promenading the deck or sitting side by side, looking out upon the moonlit waters.

"I wish I hadn't happened upon Phil Ross," Edward remarked in an undertone far from hilarious. "I fear he will, according to custom, make himself very disagreeable to you."

"I have been thinking it over, Ned," she answered, "and I have come to the conclusion that the better plan will be for you to take the first favorable opportunity to tell him of my engagement and what is the object of our journey."

"I presume such a course will be likely to save you a good deal of annoyance," Edward said. "And as we are old acquaintances, and he is evidently full of a curiosity that will assuredly lead to his asking some questions, I think it will be no difficult matter to give him the information without seeming to thrust it upon him."

At that moment Philip came up and joined them, helping himself to a seat on Elsie's other side. He seemed to be, as of old, on the best of terms with himself and very graciously disposed toward Elsie.

He, too, had been thinking of the, to him, fortunate chance (Elsie would have called it Providence) which had thrown them together where for some days they were likely to see much of each other. He had heard a report of her engagement, but refused to credit it. She had always been fond of him and it wasn't likely she would throw herself away on somebody else. And now he had come to the decision to offer her his hand, heart, and fortune without delay. He was rich enough, and why should he keep her in suspense any longer?

He indulged in a few trivial commonplaces, then invited her to take a turn with him on the deck.

But she declined with thanks and said that he must excuse her for she was greatly fatigued and must retire at once. And with a kindly "Goodnight," she withdrew to her stateroom, Edward again giving her the support of his arm.

Philip was literally struck dumb with surprise, and did not recover his speech until she was gone.

Edward returned presently and as he resumed his seat by Philip's side, the latter asked, "Is your sister out of health, Ned?"

"No, but we are just off a long and fatiguing journey. She was not at her best state either when we left home, because of the care and nursing of the sick children. And in addition to all that, she is enduring much grief and anxiety."

"May I ask on what account?"

"Yes, I have no objection to telling you the whole story, considering what old acquaintances we are, and the life-long friendship of our mothers. Lester Leland, Elsie's betrothed, is lying very ill in Rome, and we are making all haste to join him there."

"Her betrothed!" cried Philip, starting to his feet, "her betrothed did you say? Why — why, I've always expected to marry her myself! I thought it was an understood thing in both families, and —."

"I'm sure I do not know upon what grounds you entertained such an idea," returned Edward in a tone of mingled indignation and disgust.

"Grounds, man! I'm sure it would seem the most natural thing in the world — each the eldest child of intimate and dear friends — and I have never made any secret of my preference for her —."

"Which amounts to nothing unless it had been reciprocated."

"Reciprocated! I've always thought it was, and delayed speaking out plainly because I considered myself safe in waiting to grow a little richer."

"In which you were egregiously mistaken. Now let me assure you once for all, that Elsie never has and never will care for any man in that way but Lester Leland."

At that Philip turned and walked rapidly away. "I'd rather have lost all I'm worth!" he muttered to himself. "Yes, every cent of it. But as to her never caring for anybody else if that fellow was out o' the way, I don't believe it. And he may die; may be dead now. Well, if he is I'll keep a sharp look out that nobody else gets ahead of me."

His self-love and self-conceit had received a pretty deep wound; his eyes were opened to the fact that Elsie avoided being alone with him, never appearing on deck without her brother, and he did not trouble her much during the remainder of the voyage. He did not make his intended offer.

CHAPTER V

I feel
Of this dull sickness at my heart afraid:
And in my eyes the death sparks flash and fade:
And something seems to steal
Over my bosom like a frozen hand.

—WILLIS

DR. ARTHUR CONLY rode briskly up the avenue at Roselands, dismounted, throwing the bridle to a servant, and went up the steps into the veranda, whistling softly to himself.

"You seem in good spirits, Art," remarked Calhoun, who sat there with the morning paper in his hand. "I haven't heard you whistle before for — well I should say something like a fortnight."

"I am in good spirits, Cal, the Ion children are out of danger and uncle has just had a telegram from Ned announcing the safe arrival of their party to New York in good season for the steamer."

"I presume this tells the same story, though I can't think why it isn't directed to grandpa, or to me as the eldest son of the house," Calhoun said, handing an unopened telegram to his brother.

Arthur tore it hastily open, glanced at the contents and paled to the very lips.

"What is it?" cried Calhoun in alarm.

"Mother! said Arthur huskily, putting the paper into his brother's outstretched hand. "She has been struck down with apoplexy. Cal, I must take the first train for New York. Look at the paper; see when it leaves. Thank God that those children are out of danger! But I must see whom I can get to take charge of them and my other patients during my absence."

Then, calling to a servant, he directed a fresh horse to be saddled and brought to the door with all speed. Then hurrying into the house, he summoned his old mammy and bade her pack a valise with such clothing as he would need on a journey to the north that might occupy a week or more.

"You are acting very promptly," Calhoun said, following him in to give the desired information in regard to the train.

"Yes, there's not a minute to lose, Cal."

Calhoun's face was full of grief and anxiety. "I think I should go, too, Art, if — if you think there's any probability of — finding her alive."

"It's impossible to tell. But we can hardly both be spared from home. It should be kept from grandpa as long as possible, and if he saw both of us rushing off in the direction she has taken, he would know at once that something very serious had happened to her."

"Yes, you are right, and for the first time I envy you your medical knowledge and skill. She's with Virginia, the message is sent by her," glancing again at the paper which he still held in his hand. "I'm glad of that — that she has at least one of her children with her, if —."

He paused and Arthur finished the sentence. "If she will be any use or comfort to her, you were about to say? Well, we can only hope that so terrible an emergency has developed some hitherto unsuspected excellencies in Virginia's character."

A horse came galloping up the avenue. Calhoun glanced from the window.

"Another telegram!" he cried, and both brothers dashed out upon the veranda.

This was directed to Calhoun, sent from Philadelphia by their Uncle Edward Allison. He and Adelaide would be with Mrs. Conly in two hours, telegraph at once in what condition they found her, and if practicable start with her immediately for her home.

The brothers consulted together, and Arthur decided to go on with his preparations, but delay setting out upon his journey until the coming of the promised message.

It came in due time, and from it they learned that their mother was already on her way home.

The sad tidings had now to be communicated to the other near relatives, but it was deemed best to keep them from the younger children and the feeble old father until the day when she might be expected to arrive.

As gently and tenderly as possible the old gentleman's son broke the news to him.

He was much overcome. "She will never get over it, I fear," he sighed, the tears coursing down his furrowed cheeks. "One bereavement is apt to tread closely upon the heels of another, and she will probably soon follow her sister. But, oh, if I only knew that she had been washed from her sins in the precious blood of Christ. If I knew that she had accepted His invitation, 'Come unto me,' so that death would be but falling asleep in Him, safe in His arms, safe on His gentle breast — I think I could let her go almost willingly. My race is well nigh run, and it can hardly be long ere I too shall get my summons home."

"Dear father, if such be the will of God, may you be spared to us for many years yet," returned his son with emotion. "And Louise! We do not know her exact condition, but let us hope that God will, in His mercy, give her yet more time — months or years — in which to prepare for eternity. We will cry earnestly for her, and in the name of Christ, to Him who hath said, 'I have no pleasure in the death of him that dieth,' but bids them 'Turn yourselves and live ye.'"

"Yes, and whose promise is, 'If two of you shall agree on earth as touching anything they shall ask, it shall be done for them of my Father which is in heaven!'"

Silence fell between them for a moment, then the gentleman asked, "What arrangements have the boys made? She will hardly be able to drive home in a carriage."

"Oh, no! They will meet her at the depot with an

ambulance, and I shall be there with the carriage for Mr. Allison, Adelaide, and Virginia.

"Virginia is coming, too?"

"We do not know certainly, but expect to see her with the others."

"I cannot say that I hope you will. I never saw a more useless person; she will only be in the way. And — I cannot banish a suspicion that she has brought this attack upon her poor mother. I strongly suspect Virginia's match turned out a very bad one, and that she has heaped reproaches upon her mother for the hand she had in bringing it about."

"I hope not!" his son exclaimed with energy, "for if so it must surely be the cause of life-long self-reproach to her. Will you go with us to the depot, father?"

"No, no, my son! Let my first sight of my poor stricken child be where we will not be the gazing stock of an idle, curious crowd. I shall meet her here at my own door."

The train steamed into the depot and Mrs. Allison, glancing from the window of the parlor car, saw her brother and nephews standing near the track.

They saw her, too, and lifted their hats with a sad sort of smile. All felt that the invalid must be unable to sit up or her face also would have been in sight.

In another moment the train came to a stand still, and the next the three gentlemen were beside the couch on which Mrs. Conly lay.

She looked up at her sons with eyes full of intelligence, made an effort to speak, but in vain. And the big tears ran down her cheeks.

They bent over her with hearts and eyes full to overflowing.

"Mother, dear mother, we are glad you have come to us alive," Calhoun said in low, tremulous tones.

"And we hope we shall soon have you much better," added Arthur.

"Yes," said Adelaide, "she is already better than when we first saw her in New York, but has not yet recovered her speech and cannot help herself at all. One side seems to be quite paralyzed."

"We have an ambulance waiting," said Calhoun. As soon as the crowd is out of the way, it shall be brought close to the platform of this car and we will lift her into it."

Greetings were exchanged while they waited.

"Where is Virginia?" asked Mr. Dinsmore.

"She preferred to remain behind," replied Mrs. Allison in a low-toned aside, "and as she would have been of no use whatever, we did not urge her to come."

"It is just as well," was Mr. Dinsmore's comment.

Very tenderly and carefully the poor invalid was lifted and placed in the ambulance by her sons and brother. The former accompanied her in it, while the latter with Mrs. Allison, entered the Roselands family carriage and drove thither considerably in advance of the more slowly moving ambulance.

"Has Virginia made a really good match?" Mr. Dinsmore asked, addressing his sister Adelaide.

"Good! It could hardly be worse!" she exclaimed. "Would you have believed it? We found them in a tenement house, living most wretchedly."

"Is it possible? He was not wealthy then? Or has he lost his means since the marriage?"

"As far as I can learn," said Mr. Allison, "he has always lived by his wits. He is a professional gambler now."

"Dreadful! How does he treat his wife?"

"Very badly indeed, if we may credit her story. They live, as the saying is, like cat and dog, actually coming to blows at times. They are both bitterly disappointed, each having married the other merely for money, which neither had."

Mr. Dinsmore looked greatly concerned. "Virginia was never a favorite of mine," he remarked, "but I do not like to think of her as suffering from either poverty or the abusive treatment of a bad husband. Can nothing be done to better her condition?"

"I think not at the present," said Adelaide, "she has made her bed and will have to lie in it. I don't believe the man would ever proceed to personal violence if she did not exasperate him with taunts and reproaches, with slaps, scratches, and hair-pulling also, he says."

"Oh, disgraceful!" exclaimed her uncle. "I have no pity for her if she is really guilty of such conduct."

"She told me herself that on one occasion she actually threw a cup of coffee in his face in return for his accusation that she and her mother had inveigled him into the marriage by false pretenses to wealth they did not possess. Poor Louise! I have no doubt her attack was brought on by the discovery of the great mistake she and Virginia had made, and reproaches heaped on her for her share in making the match."

"'Whatsoever a man soweth, that shall he also reap,'" sighed Mr. Dinsmore. "I presume Virginia was too proud to show herself among her relatives whose approval of the match had not been asked, and acquaintances who had heard of it as a splendid affair?"

"Your conjecture is entirely correct," said Adelaide. She gave vent to her feelings on the subject in her mother's presence, supposing, I presume, as I did, that not being able to speak or move, she was also unable to hear or understand. But it was evident from the piteous expression her countenance assumed and the tears coursing down her cheeks, that she did both."

"Poor Louise! She has a sad reaping — so far as that ungrateful, undutiful daughter is concerned; but Isa, Calhoun and Arthur are of quite another stamp."

"Yes, indeed! She will surely find comfort in them. I wish Isa was not so far away. But you have not told me how my old father is. How has he borne this shock?"

"It was a shock, of course, especially to one so old and feeble; but I left him calmly staying himself upon his God."

They arrived at Roselands some time before the ambulance. They found the whole household, and also Mrs. Howard, her husband and sons, and Mrs. Travilla gathered upon the veranda to receive them.

Lora stood by her father's side and Elsie too was

very near, both full of loving care for him in this time of sore trial.

And Adelaide's first thought, first embrace, were for him. They wept a moment in each other's arms.

"Is she — is she alive?" he faltered.

"Yes, father, and we hope may get up again. Be comforted for her and for yourself, because 'He doeth all things well,' and 'We know that all things work together for good to them that love God.'"

"Yes, yes, and who can tell but this may be His appointed means of bringing her into the fold!"

There had been time for an exchange of greetings all around and a few comforting words to the younger Conlys when the ambulance was seen entering the avenue.

With beating hearts and tearful eyes they watched its slow progress. Lying helpless and speechless in the shadow of death, Louise Conly seemed nearer and dearer than ever before to father, children, brothers and sisters.

The ambulance stopped close to the veranda steps, and the same strong, loving arms that had placed her in it now lifted her anew and bore her into the house, the other looking on in awed and tearful silence.

She was carried to her own room, laid upon the bed, and one by one, they stood for an instant at her side with a kiss of welcome.

It was evident that she knew them all, though able to speak only with those sad, wistful eyes that gazed with new yearning affection into the faces of father and children.

But presently Arthur, by virtue of his medical authority, banished them all from the room except Lora, Elsie and a faithful and attached old Negress who had lived all her days in the family and was a competent nurse.

CHAPTER VI

Then come the wild weather - come sleet or come snow,
We will stand by each other, however it blow;
Oppression and sickness, and sorrow and pain,
Shall be to our true love as links to a chain.

—LONGFELLOW (FROM THE GERMAN)

"COURAGE, SISTER DEAR!" whispered Edward Travilla, putting an arm tenderly about Elsie's waist as they found themselves at the very door of Lester Leland's studio.

Her face had grown very pale and she was trembling with agitation.

Still supporting her with his arm, Edward rapped gently upon the door. At the same instant it was opened from within by the attending physician, who had just concluded his morning call upon his patient.

He was an Italian of gentlemanly appearance and intelligent countenance.

"Some friends of Signor Leland from America?" he said in good English and with a polite bow.

"Yes, how is he?" Edward asked, stepping in and drawing his sister on with him.

"Sick, signor, very sick, but he will grow better now. I shall expect to see him up in a few weeks," the doctor answered with a significant glance and smile as he turned, with a second and still lower bow, to the sweet, fair maiden.

She did not see it, for her eyes were roving round the room — a disorderly and comfortless place, but garnished with some gems of art. An unfinished picture was on the easel. There were others with their faces to the wall. Models, statues in various stages of completion, and the implements of painter and sculptor were scattered here and there. A screen, an old lounge, a few chairs, and a table littered with books, papers, and drawing materials completed the furniture of the large, dreary apartment.

An open door gave a glimpse into an inner room, from which came a slight sound as of restless movement, a sigh or groan.

Pointing to the chairs, the physician invited the strangers to be seated.

Edward put his sister in one and took possession of another close at her side.

"How soon can we see Mr. Leland?" he asked, putting his card into the doctor's hand.

"I will go and prepare Signor Leland for the interview," the doctor answered and disappeared through the open doorway.

"Good news for you signor!" they heard him say in a quiet tone.

"Ah! Let me have it," sighed a well-known voice. " 'As cold water to a thirsty soul, so is good news from a far country.' "

"You are right, signor, it comes from far off America. A friend — a young signor has arrived and asked to see you."

"Ah! His name?" exclaimed the sick man, with a tremor of gladness in his feeble tones.

"Here is his card."

" 'Edward Travilla!' — Ah, what joy! Let me see him at once. 'Twill be like a breath of home air!' "

Every word had reached the ears of the two in the studio.

"Go! Go!" cried Elsie, scarcely above her breath, and Edward rose and went softly in.

"Not much talk now, signores," Elsie heard the doctor say.

"No, we'll be prudent," Edward said, grasping Lester's hand.

"So good! So kind! More than I dared hope! But how

is she? My darling?" Elsie heard in feeble, faltering yet eager accents."

"Well, very well, and longing to come here and nurse you back to health.

"Ah, a glimpse of her sweet face I think would bring me back from the borders of the grave! But I could not expect or ask such a sacrifice."

Elsie could wait no longer; she rose and glided with swift, almost noiseless steps to the bedside.

Edward made way for her. Lester looked up, caught sight of her, and a flash of exceeding joy lighted up his pale, emaciated features.

"Elsie!"

"Lester!"

She dropped to her knees, laid her face on the pillow beside his and their lips met in a long kiss.

"Oh, love, love! How sweet, how kind, how dear of you!" he murmured.

"I have come to be your nurse," she said, with a lovely blush and smile, "come to stay with you always while God spares our lives."

Soon Edward went out and left them together. He had much to attend to, with Ben and Dinah as helpers. Other and better apartments were speedily rented, cleaned, and comfortably, even elegantly furnished. Their mother had sent them off with full purses and carte blanche to draw upon her bankers for further supplies as they might be needed. And Edward knew it would be her desire to see Elsie and Lester surrounded by the luxuries to which she had been accustomed from her birth.

When night came the doctor pronounced his patient already wonderfully improved.

"But the signora must leave him to me and the nurse tonight," he said. "She is fatigued with her long journey and must take her rest and sleep, or she too will be ill."

So Elsie took possession of the pleasant room which had been prepared for her, and casting on the Lord all care for herself and dear ones, and full of glad anticipations for the future, slept long and sweetly.

It was early morning when she woke. That day and several succeeding ones were spent at Lester's side in the gentle ministrations love teaches. There was little talk between them, for he was very weak, and love needs few words. But he slept much of the time with her hand in his, and waking gazed tenderly, joyously into the sweet face.

Happiness proved the best of medicines, and every hour brought a slight increase of strength, a change for the better in all the symptoms.

Meanwhile, Edward and the two servants were busy laying in needed supplies and the preparation of the suite of apartments which were to form the new home — Elsie giving a little oversight and direction.

At length their labors were completed, and she was called in to take a critical survey and point out any deficiency, if such there were.

She could find none. "My dear brother, how can I thank you enough?" she said with a look of grateful affection.

"You are satisfied?"

"Oh, entirely! I only wish mamma and the rest could see how comfortable, tasteful, really beautiful you have made these rooms!"

"I am very glad our work pleases you. And the doctor tells me that under the combined influence of good nursing and unexpected happiness, Lester is gaining faster than he could have deemed possible. What is the time fixed upon for the ceremony which is to rob you of your last name, sister mine?"

"Add to it, you should say," she corrected with a charming blush. "Noon of day after tomorrow is the hour. Edward, do you know that our good doctor is a Waldensian?"

"No, I did not, and am pleased to learn it; though I was satisfied that he was no Papist."

"Yes, he is one of that long-persecuted noble race, and will take you to see his pastor on our behalf. I have so greatly admired and loved the Waldenses that I really feel that to be married by one of their pastors will be some small compensation for — for being so far from home and — mamma. Oh, Edward, if she were but here!"

Her tears were falling fast. He put his arm about her waist, her head dropped upon his shoulder and he smoothed her hair with a caressing hand.

"It is hard for you," he said tenderly, "so different from what you and all of us have looked forward to. But you have been very brave, dear; and what a blessing that your coming is working such a cure for Lester!"

"Yes, oh, yes! God is very good to me, His blessings are unnumbered!"

"It seems a sad sort of wedding for you," he said, "but I shall telegraph the hour to mamma immediately, and they will all be thinking of and praying for you."

"Oh, that is a comfort I had not thought of!" she exclaimed, with glad tears shining in her eyes. "What a blessing you are to me, brother dear!"

Lester was not able to leave his bed or likely to be for weeks, but that she might devote herself the more entirely to him, Elsie had consented to be married at once.

She laid aside her mourning for the occasion, and Dinah helped her to array herself for her wedding in a very beautiful evening dress of some white material, which had been worn, but once before.

"Pity dars no time to get a new dress, Miss Elsie," remarked the handmaiden half regretfully. "Doe sho' nuff you couldn't look no sweeter and beautifuller dan you does in dis."

"I prefer this, Dinah, because they all — even dear, dear papa — have seen me in it," Elsie said, hastily wiping away a tear. "And I remember he said it became me well. Oh, I can see his proud, fond smile as he said it, and almost feel the touch of his lips, for he bent down and kissed me so tenderly."

"Miss Elsie, I jes b'lieves he's a lookin' at you now dis bressed minute, and ef de res' of dose dat lubs you is far away he'll be sho to stan' close side o' you when de ministah's a saying de words dat make you Massa Leland's wife."

"Ah, Dinah, what a sweet thought! And who shall say it may not be so!"

"Dar's Massa Ed'ard!" exclaimed Dinah, as a quick, manly step was heard followed by a light rap upon the door.

She hastened to open it. "We's ready, Marse Ed'ard."

He did not seem to hear or heed her. His eyes were fastened upon his beautiful sister, more beautiful at this moment, he thought, than ever before.

"Elsie!" he cried. "Oh that mamma could see you! She herself could hardly have been a lovelier bride! Yet these are wanted to complete your attire," opening a box he had brought and taking therefrom a veil of exquisite texture and design and a wreath of orange blossoms.

"How kind and thoughtful, Edward!" she said, thanking him with a sweet though tearful smile, "but are they suitable for such a wedding as this?"

"Surely," he said. "Come, Dinah, and help me to arrange them."

Their labors finished, he stepped back a little to note the effect.

"Oh, darling sister," he exclaimed, "never, I am sure, was there a lovelier bride! I wish the whole world could see   you!"

"Our own little world at Ion is all I should ask for," she responded in tremulous tones.

"Yes, it must be very hard for you," he said, "especially not to have mamma here, you who have always clung to her so closely. Such a different wedding as it is from hers! But it's very romantic, you know," he added jocosely, trying to raise her drooping spirits.

"Ah, I am forgetting a piece of news I have to tell. I met an American gentleman and his daughter the other day, fell into conversation with him, and learned that we have several common acquaintances. I think we were mutually pleased, and I have asked him and his daughter in to the wedding — thinking it would not be unpleasant to you, and we should thus have two more witnesses."

"Perhaps it is best we should," she returned, in her sweet, gentle way, yet looking somewhat disturbed.

"I'm afraid I ought to have consulted you first," he said. "I'm sorry, but it is too late now. His name is Love; his daughter — an extremely pretty girl by the way — he calls Zoe."

Ben now came to the door to say that all was in readiness — the minister, the doctor, and the other gentleman and a lady had arrived.

Edward gave his arm to his sister and led her into the room, to which Lester had been carried a few moments before, and where he lay on a luxurious couch, propped up with pillows into a half-sitting posture.

A touch of color came into his pale cheeks, and his eyes shone with love and joy as they rested upon his lovely bride, as Edward led her to the side of the couch.

Dinah and Ben followed, taking their places near the door and watching the proceedings with interest and sympathy.

The minister stood up, the doctor, the stranger guests, the nurse also, and the ceremony began.

Elsie's eyes were full of tears, but her sweet low tones were distinct and clear as she took the marriage vows.

So were Lester's — his voice seemed stronger than it had been for weeks and when he took the small white-gloved hand in his, the grasp was firm as well as tender.

"One kiss, my love, my wife!" he pleaded when the ceremony was ended.

A soft blush suffused the fair face and neck, but the request was granted. She bent over him and for an instant their lips met.

Then Edward embraced her with brotherly affection and good wishes. He grasped Lester's hand in cordial greeting, then turned and introduced his newly made friends to the bride and groom.

A table loaded with delicacies stood in an adjoining room, and thither the brother and sister and their guests now repaired, while for a short season the invalid was left to quietness and repose that he might recover from the unusual excitement and fatigue.

Chapter VII

Therein he them full fair did entertain,
Not with such forged shows as fitter been
For courting fools, that courtesies would faine,
But with entire affection plain.

—Spenser's Fairy Queen

ONE BRIGHT MORNING in November the Ion family were gathered about the breakfast table. Rosie and Walter were there for the first time since their severe illness, a trifle pale and thin still, but nearly in usual health, and very glad to be permitted to take their old places at the table.

Mrs. Dinsmore had returned from her sojourn at the Laurels, the home of her daughter Rose. The grandchildren there, whom she had been nursing, had also recovered their health, and so the places of the eldest son and daughter of the house were the only vacant ones.

Both Elsie and Edward were sorely missed, especially by the mother and Violet.

"It seems time we had letters again from our absentees, papa," Mrs. Travilla remarked as she poured the coffee. "We have had none since the telegram giving the hour of the wedding."

"No, but perhaps we may hear this morning — the mail has not yet come."

"Yes, grandpa, here come Solon with it," said Harold, glancing away from the window.

In a few moments the man came in bringing the mailbag, which he handed to Mr. Dinsmore.

All looked up with interest, the younger ones in eager expectation, while their grandfather opened it and examined the contents.

"Yes, daughter, there is a letter from each of them, both directed to you," he said, glancing over the addresses on several letters which he now held in his hand. "Here, Tom," to the servant in waiting, "take these to your mistress. Don't read them to the neglecting of your breakfast," he added with a smile, again addressing Mrs. Travilla.

"No, sir, they will keep," she answered, returning the smile. "And you shall all share the pleasure of their perusal with me after prayers. Doubtless they give the particulars we all want so much to learn."

They all gathered round her at the appointed time. She held the letters open in her hand, having already given them a cursory examination lest there should be some little confidence intended for none but "mother's" eye.

"Papa," she said, looking up half tearfully, half smiling at him as he stood at her side, "the deed is done, and another claims my first-born darling as his own."

"You have not lost her, Elsie dearest, but have gained a son; and I trust we shall have them both with us ere long," he responded, bending down to touch his lips to the brow still as smooth and fair as in the days of her girlhood.

"Poor, dear Elsie! How she must have missed and longed for you, dearest mamma!" Violet sighed, kneeling close to her mother's chair and putting her arms around her.

"What is it? All about Elsie's wedding?" asked Herbert. "Please let us hear it, mamma. The telegram told nothing but the hour when it was to be, and I was so surprised, for I never understood that that was what she went away for."

"Nor I," said Harold, "though I suppose it was very stupid in us not to understand."

"Who did get married with my sister Elsie, mamma?" asked little Walter.

"Mr. Leland, my son."

"But I thought he was most dead," remarked Rosie in surprise.

"He has been very ill," her mother said, "but is improving fast, though not yet able to sit up."

Rosie, opening her eyes wide in astonishment, was beginning another question when Harold stopped her.

"Wait, Rosie, don't you see mamma is going to read the letters? They will tell us all about it, I presume."

"I shall read Edward's first. It gives a very minute account of what they have done since he wrote last, just after their arrival in Rome," the mother said. "He is a good boy to take the trouble to tell us everything in detail, is he not, papa?"

"Yes," Mr. Dinsmore assented, seating himself by her side and taking Rosie upon one knee, Walter on the other. "And so good a mother richly deserves good, thoughtful sons and daughters, ever ready to do all in their power to promote her happiness or afford her pleasure. Does she not, children?"

"Yes, grandpa, indeed she does!" they replied in chorus.

Her sweet soft eyes glistened with happy tears as she sent a loving glance round the little circle. Then, all becoming perfectly quiet and attentive, she began to read.

Edward's first item of news was that the marriage had just taken place; the next that Lester's health was steadily improving. Then came a description of the rooms they were occupying — both as they were when first seen by Elsie and himself and as they had become under his renovating and improving hands.

After that he drew a vivid picture of Elsie's appearance in her bridal robes, told who were present at the ceremony, who performed it, how the several actors acquitted themselves, and what refreshments were served after it was over.

He said he thought happiness was working a rapid cure with Lester, and that from all he could see and hear, his success as both a painter and sculptor was already assured.

Elsie's themes were the same, but she had much to say of Edward's kind thoughtfulness, his energy and helpfulness — "The best and kindest of brothers," she called him, and as she read the words the mother's eyes shone with love and pride in her eldest son.

But her voice trembled, and the tears had to be wiped away once and again when she came to that part of the letter in which Elsie told of her feelings as she robed herself for her wedding with none to assist but Dinah. How sad was her heart, dearly as she loved Lester, and how full of longing for home and mother and all the dear ones so far away. Then she told of the comfort she found in the idea that possibly her dear departed father might be near her in spirit.

"Was it wrong, mamma," she asked, "to think he might perhaps be allowed to be a ministering spirit to me in my loneliness? And to take pleasure in the thought?"

"Mamma, what do you think about it?" asked Herbert.

"I don't know that we have any warrant for the idea in the Scriptures," she answered. "It seems to be one of the things that is not revealed. Yet, I see no harm in taking comfort in the thought that it may be so. My poor lonely darling! I am glad she had that consolation. Ah, papa, what a different wedding from mine!"

"Yes," he said, "and from what we thought hers would be. But I trust she will never see cause to regret the step she has taken. Lester is worth saving even at the sacrifice she has made."

His daughter looked at him with glistening eyes. "Thank you, papa, that is a good thought, and consoles me greatly for both our darling and ourselves."

She went on with the reading of the letter. There were but a few more sentences. Then, while the others discussed its contents, Violet stole quietly from the room, unobserved as she thought. But in that she was mistaken. Her mother's eyes followed her with a look of love and sympathy.

"Dear child!" she said in a low aside to her father, "she misses Elsie sorely. I sometimes think almost more than I do. They were so inseparable and so strongly attached."

Vi's heart was very full, for Elsie's marriage, though

far, far from being so great a sorrow as the death of their father, seemed in some respects even more the breaking up of a life that had been very sweet.

She sought the studio she and Elsie had shared together (how lonely and deserted it seemed!) and there gave vent to her feelings in a burst of tears.

"Oh, Elsie, darling! We were so happy together! Such dear friends! With never a disagreement, hardly a thought unshared! And now I am alone! All alone!

She had unconsciously spoken aloud. A soft sweet voice echoed the word.

"Alone! Ah, my darling, no! Not while your mother lives. You and I must cling the closer together, Vi dearest," the voice went on, while two loving arms enfolded her and a gentle kiss was imprinted upon cheek and brow.

"Dearest mamma!" cried Violet, returning the caress, "forgive me that I should indulge in such grief while you are left me — you and your dear love, the greatest of earthly treasures."

"Yes, dear child, your grief is very natural. These changes, though not unmixed calamities, are one of the hard conditions of life in this world, dear daughter. But we must not let them mar our peace and happiness. Let us rejoice over the blessings that are left, rather than weep for those that are gone."

"I will, mamma," Violet said, wiping away her tears. "Ah, how much I still have to rejoice in and be thankful for!"

"Yes, dear, we both have! And not the least is the love of Him who has said, 'Lo, I am with you always.' Oh the joy, the bliss of knowing that nothing can ever part us from Him! And then to know, too, that some day we shall all be together in His immediate presence, beholding His face and bearing His image!"

Neither spoke again for some moments, then the mother said, "Vi, dearest, there is nothing more conducive to cheerfulness at such a time as this than being fully employed. So I ask you to take charge of Rosie and Walter for a few hours. They are not yet well enough for tasks or for out-of-door sports but need to be amused.

And your grandpa and grandma want me to drive with them to the Laurels and Roselands."

"Yes, do go, mamma, and try to enjoy yourself. You have seen so little of Aunt Adelaide since she came, or of Aunt Rosie, since the sickness began with her children and ours. Thank you for your trust; I shall do my best." Violet said with cheerful alacrity. "Ah, the recovery of the darlings is one of the many mercies we have to be thankful for!"

"Yes, Vi, and my heart is full of joy and gratitude to the Great Physician."

At Roselands, Mrs. Conly still lay helpless on her couch, her condition having changed very slightly for the better. She could now at times, with great effort, speak a word or two, but friends and physicians had scarcely a hope of any further improvement. She might live on thus for years, or another stroke might at any moment bring the end.

Cut off from all means of communicating her thoughts and feelings, she could show them only by the expression of her countenance, which was sullen, fierce, despairing, piteous by turn.

She had the best of care and nursing from her sisters, her sons, and her old mammy, assisted occasionally by other friends and relatives, and could not fail to read in their faces and the tones of their voices tender pity and sympathy for her in her sore affliction.

They could not tell whether she understood all that was said to her, but hoping that she did, spoke often to her of the loving Savior and tried to lead her to Him.

Hitherto the Ion friends had not been able to be with her a great deal, but it had not been necessary as Adelaide was still at Roselands.

She, however, expected soon to return to her own home, and there would then be greater need of their services. Therefore, there was double reason for thankfulness for the restoration to health of the little ones at Ion and the Laurels, releasing, as it did, both Mrs.

Dinsmore and Mrs. Travilla from the cares and labors which had occupied them for some weeks past.

The latter gave expression to that thought while driving to the Laurels with her father and his wife adding, "I can now hold myself in readiness to take Aunt Adelaide's place at any moment."

"Not with my consent," said Mr. Dinsmore emphatically. "If you consider yourself at all under my authority you will take a week at least of entire rest and relaxation."

She looked at him with her own sweet smile, full of filial love and reverence, and putting her hand in is, said, "Yes, my dear father, that is still one of my great happinesses, as it has been almost ever since I can remember. Ah, it is often very restful to me just to resign myself to your wise, loving guidance and control!"

His fingers closed over the small, daintily gloved hand, holding it in a warm and tender clasp.

"Then do not forget that you are not to undertake anything that can tax your strength, without my knowledge and permission. Nor must you, Rose," he added with playful authority, turning an affectionate, smiling glance upon her. "You too are worn out and must have some rest."

"Well, my dear," she said laughingly, "I make no rash promises. You know I never have equaled Elsie in submissiveness."

"No, and yet you have usually shown yourself amenable to authority."

"Perhaps because it has so seldom been exerted," she saucily returned. "My dear, we have not yet had our first quarrel."

"And have lived together for thirty odd years. I think it would hardly be worth while to begin after so long a delay."

"Nor do I," she said, "therefore, I shall probably yield to your wishes in this matter — or commands — call them what you will, especially as they are in full accord with my own inclinations."

"Elsie," he said, turning to his daughter again, "I have taken the liberty of inviting some guests to Ion this morning."

"Liberty, papa!" she exclaimed. "It would be impossible for you to take liberties with me or mine. I consider your rights and authority in any house of mine fully equal, if not superior to my own. If the mistress of the mansion be subject to your control," she added, with a bright look up into his face, and much of the old time archness in her smile, "surely all else must be."

"Thank you daughter. Then I have not taken a liberty, but I have invited the guests all the same. You do not ask how it happened or who they are, but I proceed to explain. In glancing over the morning paper, while you and Rose were dressing for the drive, I saw among the items of news that Donald Keith is in our city. So I dispatched Solon with a carriage and a hastily written note asking Donald to come out to see us, bringing with him any friend or friends he might choose."

"I am glad you did, papa; they shall have a warm welcome. But will it not make it necessary for us to return home earlier than we intended?"

"No, not at all. It is not likely they will arrive until near our dinner hour — if they come at all today. And if they should be there earlier, Violet is quite capable of entertaining them."

"Yes," said Mrs. Dinsmore, "I know of no one more competent to minister to the enjoyment of either grown people or children. As regards talent, sweetness of disposition, and utter unselfishness combined, our Vi is one in a thousand."

"Thank you, mamma, for saying it," Elsie said, her eyes shining with pleasure. "She seems all that to me, but I thought it might be that mother love magnified her good qualities and made me blind to her imperfections."

Violet, in the nursery at home, was showing herself worthy of this praise by her efforts to amuse the little ones and keep them from missing the dear mother who had been so constantly with them of late. She played quiet little games with them, told them beautiful stories, showed them pictures and drew others for them, dressed dolls for Rosie and cut paper horses for Walter.

Several hours were passed thus, then seeing them begin to look weary — for they were still weak from their recent illness — she coaxed them to lie down while she sang them to sleep.

The closed eyes and soft breathing telling that they slept, she rose and bent over them a moment, gazing tenderly into each little face, then drawing out her watch and turning to the old nurse whispered, "It is time for me to dress for dinner, mammy. I'll go now, but if they wake and want me let me know at once."

Her dressing was scarcely completed when the sound of wheels caught her ears.

"There! Mamma has come! Dear, dear mamma!" she said half aloud, and presently hastened from the room to meet and welcome her.

But instead a servant was coming leisurely up the broad stairway.

"Where is mamma, Prilla?" the young girl asked in a slightly disappointed tone.

"Miss Elsie not come yet, Miss Wilet. De gentlemen is in de drawing room," Prilla answered, handing her two visiting cards to her young mistress.

"'Donald Keith, U.S.A.,'" read Violet with a brightening countenance, as she glanced at the first. On the other was inscribed L. Raymond, U.S.N.

Violet hastening to the drawing room, met her cousin with outstretched hand and cordial greeting.

"I am glad you have come, Cousin Donald! We have all wanted you to see Ion."

"Thank you Cousin Violet. You can't have wished it more than I, I am sure," he said with a look of delight. "Allow me to introduce my friend, Captain Raymond, of the Navy. You see, I took your grandfather at his word and brought a friend with me."

Violet had already given her hand to her cousin's friend — as such he must have no doubtful welcome —

but at Donald's concluding sentence she turned to him again with a look of surprised inquiry. He was about to answer, when the door opened and Mr. Dinsmore, his wife and daughter came in.

There were fresh greetings and introductions, Mr. Dinsmore saying, as he shook hands with the guests, "So you received my hasty note, Donald, and accepted for yourself and a friend? That was right. You are both most welcome, and we hope will find Ion pleasant enough to be willing to prolong your stay and to desire to visit us again."

"Thank you, I was certain of that before I came," said Donald.

"And surely am now that I am here," remarked the captain gallantly, and with an admiring glance from Mrs. Dinsmore's still bright and comely face to the more beautiful ones of Elsie and her daughter.

Elsie's beauty had not faded. She was still young and fair in appearance, with the same sweetly pure and innocent expression which old Mrs. Dinsmore had been wont to stigmatize as "that babyish look." And Violet's face was peerless in its fresh young beauty.

As for the captain himself, he was a man of commanding presence, noble countenance, and magnificent physique, with fine dark eyes and an abundance of dark brown curling hair and beard. Evidently Donald's senior by some years, yet not looking much, if at all, over thirty.

The two older ladies presently left the room to reappear shortly in dinner dress.

While they were gone Mr. Dinsmore engaged the captain in conversation, and Donald and Violet talked together in a low aside.

"Your sister is well, I hope?" he remarked interrogatively.

"Elsie? We had letters from her and Edward this morning. They were well at the time of writing."

"They are not at home then?" he said in a tone of surprise and disappointment.

"Oh, no! Had you not heard?" and Violet's eyes filled. "It is very foolish, I'm afraid," she went on in half tremulous tones, in answer to his inquiring look, "but I can't help feeling that Lester Leland has robbed me of my sister."

"She is married? And has gone to a home of her own?"

Violet answered by telling the story as succinctly as possible.

"He was in Italy pursuing his art studies," she said. "They had become engaged shortly before he went, and a few weeks ago we heard he was very ill with typhoid fever. Elsie at once said she must go to him, she could not let him die for lack of good nursing. So grandpa and mamma consented to her going with Edward and our faithful old Ben — papa's favorite servant, who traveled for years with him in Europe — for protectors.

"Of course, she took a maid too, and Aunt Louise offered to go with them, but was taken sick in New York, so had to be left behind.

"They found Lester very but not hopelessly ill, and the joy of seeing them had an excellent effect. So they were married, Cousin Donald. Just think how sad for poor Elsie! Away from mamma and all of us except Edward!"

"It was sad for her, I am sure!" he said with warm sympathy, "and very, very noble and unselfish in her to leave all for him."

"Yes, and yet not more, I think, than any right-minded woman would do for the man she loved well enough to marry."

Harold and Herbert came in at that moment full of boyish enthusiasm and delight over the arrival of "Cousin Donald," whom they liked and admired extremely — especially for his fine figure, soldierly bearing, and pleasant, kindly manner.

They had hardly done shaking hands with him and Captain Raymond, to whom their grandfather introduced them with a look of parental pride, when their mother and "Grandma Rose" returned to the drawing room and dinner was announced.

CHAPTER VIII

*A man's heart deviseth his way;
but the Lord directeth his steps.*

—PROVERBS 16:9

THE BOYS WERE greatly disappointed on learning from the talk at the dinner table that Cousin Donald's furlough was so short that he could give but two days to his Ion friends.

There were many expressions of regret. Then Mr. Dinsmore said, "If you must leave us so soon, we must make good use of our time by taking you at once to see relatives, friends, and places of interest in the neighborhood. If you and the captain are not too weary to enjoy a ride or drive, we will go to Roselands for a call this afternoon, then on to the Oaks to take tea with my son Horace and his family."

"You can assure us of a welcome at both places?" Donald said inquiringly and with a slight smile.

"You need not have the slightest fear on that score," was the quick, earnest rejoinder.

"I for one," remarked the captain, "am not in the least fatigued, and if the ladies are to be of the party, accept with pleasure and thanks."

"I also," said Donald, with a look at Violet which seemed to express a hope that she was not intending to remain behind.

Mrs. Dinsmore and Mrs. Travilla excused themselves from going on the plea of fatigue from recent nursing of the sick and the long drive of the morning, Elsie adding that her little convalescents ought hardly to be deprived of mamma all day.

"Then we will take Vi," said Mr. Dinsmore, looking affectionately at her. "She has shut herself up with those same convalescents all the morning and needs air and exercise."

"Yes, papa," her mother said, "and I know she would enjoy a gallop on her favorite pony. Cousin," turning to Donald, "we have both riding and carriage horses at your and the captain's service. Please, do not hesitate to express your preference."

They thanked her, and after a little more discussion it was arranged that the whole party, including Harold and Herbert, should ride.

The horses were ordered at once and they set out very shortly after leaving the table. Mr. Dinsmore and the captain headed the cavalcade, Donald and Violet came next, riding side by side, and the two lads brought up the rear.

Donald was well satisfied with the arrangement, and he and Vi found a good deal of enjoyment in recalling scenes, doings, and happenings of the past summer — particularly of the weeks spent together on the New Jersey coast.

Also, Vi rehearsed to him Edward's account of Elsie's wedding and his description of the suite of apartments he had had fitted up for their use. Edward expected to spend the winter there, she said.

It was all very interesting to Donald. He thought Lester Leland a man to be envied, yet perhaps less so than he who should secure for his own the fair, sweet maiden riding by his side.

They passed a pleasant hour at Roselands, seeing all the family except the invalid, then rode on to the Oaks, where they found a warm welcome and most delightful and hospitable entertainment.

Then the return to Ion by moonlight was very enjoyable.

It was still early when they arrived. The two older ladies awaited them in the parlor, and some time was spent in pleasant conversation before retiring for the night.

"I have not yet had the pleasure of seeing my little favorites, Rosie and Walter, Cousin Elsie," remarked Donald.

"No," she said, "and they are very eager for time with you. They are in bed now, but I hope they will be well enough to join us at breakfast tomorrow."

"They have been quite sick?"

"Yes, dangerously ill for a time, and though about again, still need constant care lest they should take cold."

The guests, given adjoining rooms, opened the door of communication between and had a little private chat together before seeking their pillows.

"These relatives of yours, Keith, are extremely nice people," remarked the captain.

"Of course they are," returned Donald, "relatives to be proud of."

"I never saw a more beautiful woman than Mrs. Travilla," pursued the captain. "I think I may say never one so beautiful, and the most charming part of it is beauty that will last — beauty of heart and intellect. Can she be Miss Violet's own mother? There is a resemblance, though their styles of beauty are quite different, but there does not seem to be sufficient difference in age."

"She is her own mother, though, and not only Violet, but to two older ones — a son and daughter."

The captain expressed great surprise. "But youthful looks must be a family characteristic," he added meditatively. "Mr. and Mrs. Dinsmore look extremely young to be the grandparents of the family."

Donald explained that Mr. Dinsmore was really only eighteen years older than his daughter, and Rose, a second wife, but half as many.

"And what think you of Violet's beauty?" he asked.

"Absolutely faultless! She has an angelic face! If I were a young fellow like you, Keith, I'd certainly not look elsewhere while I could see a ray of hope in that direction. But there's the relationship in the way."

"It's too distant to stand in the way," returned Donald a trifle shortly. "I look upon her prospective wealth as a far greater obstacle, having no fancy for playing the role of fortune hunter or laying myself open to the suspicion of being such."

"Then you've no intention of trying for her?"

"I haven't said so, have I? Well, goodnight, it's getting late."

"What do you think of Captain Raymond?" Rose asked her husband. "You have had by far the best opportunity to cultivate his acquaintance."

"He impresses me very favorably as both a man and a Christian," was the emphatic reply.

"Ah, I am glad Donald has so nice a friend," was her pleased comment.

"Yes, there seems a warm friendship existing between them, though the captain must be older by several years. Married, too, for he mentioned his children incidentally."

On coming down to the parlor the next morning, the guests found Mr. Dinsmore there caressing his little grandchildren — Rosie on one knee, Walter on the other.

Cousin Donald's entrance was hailed with delight; Walter presently transferred to his knee.

Then the captain coaxed Rosie to his, saying, "Your dark eyes and hair remind me of my little Lulu's."

"Have you a little girl of your own, sir?" Rosie asked with a look of interest.

"Yes, my dear, two of them. Lulu is a year or two younger than I take you to be, and Gracie is only seven."

"Have you any boys?" inquired Walter.

"Yes, my little man, I have one. We call him Max. He is two years older than Lulu."

"About as old as I am?" said Rosie half inquiringly.

"Yes, if you are eleven as I suppose."

"Yes, sir, I'm eleven and Walter's five."

"If they're good children, we'd like 'em to come here and play with us," remarked Walter.

"I am afraid they are not always good," the captain said with a smile and a half sigh. "I am not with them enough to give them the teaching and training that doubtless you enjoy."

"But why doesn't their mamma do it? Our mamma teaches us," and the child's eyes turned lovingly upon her as at that moment she entered the room.

The usual morning greetings were exchanged, and Walter's question remained unanswered.

The gentlemen were out nearly all day, riding or driving. The ladies were with them a part of the time. The evening was enlivened with music and conversation, and all retired to rest at a seasonable hour, the two guests expecting to take leave of their hospitable entertainers the next morning.

Darkness and silence reigned for some hours; then, the shining of a bright light into Donald's eyes awoke him.

He sprang from his bed, rushed to the window, saw that a cottage not far away, which he had noticed in riding by, was in flames. The next moment he snatched up a few articles of clothing and was at the captain's side shaking him vigorously.

"Up, Raymond! Up, man! There's a fire and we'll be needed to help put it out."

"What is it? Breakers ahead, do you say?" muttered the captain, only half awake.

"Fire! Fire!" repeated Keith.

"Fire? Where?" and the captain sprang up, now wide-awake, and began hurrying on his clothes.

"That cottage down the road."

"That's bad indeed, but not quite so bad as a vessel foundering or burning at sea. Anybody else in the house awake?"

"I don't know. Yes, there! I hear steps and voices."

They hurried into the hall and down the stairs. Mr. Dinsmore was in the lower hall giving directions to the men servants who were all collected there.

"Haste! Solon, Tom, Dick — all of you!" he was saying, "gather up all the large buckets about the house, ropes too and ladders, and follow me as fast as you can. Ah, captain and Donald, too! You have seen the fire, I suppose? Will you come with me? There'll be work enough for us all no doubt. We've no engine in this neighborhood."

"Certainly, sir!"

"That's the port we are bound for." And each catching up a bucket they all three set off at full speed in the direction of the burning house, several of the Negroes following close at their heels.

They found a crowd already gathered there — men and women, black and white. Some were carrying out furniture from the lower rooms, some bringing water in buckets from a spring near by, others contenting themselves with looking on and giving orders that nobody obeyed.

"I see the house will have to go," Mr. Dinsmore said. "Are the family all out of it?"

"All but an old colored woman," some one replied, "old Aunt Betsy. Nobody thought of her in time, and now it's too late, for the stairs are burned away. Hark!" as a crash was heard, "there's the last of them."

"What! Will you leave a helpless old woman to be burned alive?" cried Captain Raymond. "Where is she?"

"Yonder!" cried several voices. "See, she's at the window! And she's screaming for help!" as a wild shriek rent the air, a black face full of terror and despair showing itself at an upper window, where the fire's lurid light fell full upon it.

"Oh, ain't dar nobody to help ole Aunt Betsy?" she screamed, stretching out her wrinkled arms and toil-worn hands in passionate entreaty. "Will you ebery one ob you leave de po' ole woman to burn up in dis awful fiah? Isn't yo' got no pity in yo' souls? Oh, somebody come an' help de po' ole woman to git down 'fore she burn all up!"

"A rope!" shouted the captain. "Quick! Quick! A rope!"

"Heah, massa cap'n!" answered Solon close at hand. "I'se brung it jus' in time."

"What can you do with a rope, Raymond?" asked Donald.

"Make an effort to save her with the help of that lightening rod."

~ 69 ~

"You risk your own life, and it is worth far more than hers," Donald said entreatingly.

"Stay a moment, captain," said Mr. Dinsmore, "they are bringing a ladder."

"But there's no time to lose. See, the flames are already bursting out from the next window!"

"Yes, but here it is," as the Negroes halted with it close beside them. "It is to be used to reach that window, boys," he said, turning to them and pointing upward. "Set it up there."

"Can't do it sah! Mos' as much as a man's life is wuth to go so near de fire."

"Then give it to me!" cried the captain, taking hold of it, Mr. Dinsmore and Donald giving their assistance.

It was the work of a moment to set it up against the wall. In another the captain was ascending it, while the other two held it firmly in place.

He gained the window and sprang in.

"Bress you, massa! Bress you!" exclaimed the old Negress, "you's gwine to save me I knows."

"Get out here on to the ladder and climb down as fast as you can," he said hurriedly, taking hold of her arm to help her.

"But she drew back shuddering, "I can't, massa! I'se ole and stiff. I can't no how 'tall."

There was not a moment to lose. The captain stepped back on to the top round of the ladder, took her in his arms, and began as rapid a descent as was possible so burdened.

The ladder shook beneath their weight, for both were heavy, and Aunt Betsy struggled in his grasp, screaming with fright. Then a tongue of flame shooting out from below caught her cotton gown, and in her frantic terror she gave a sudden spring that threw her preserver and herself to the ground.

Mr. Dinsmore and Donald seized the captain and dragged him out of harm's way, other hands doing the same service for the woman.

She was shrieking and groaning, but her rescuer neither spoke nor moved.

They took him up, carried him out of the crowd, and laid him gently down upon a sofa — one of the articles of furniture saved from the fire.

"Poor fellow!" sighed Donald with emotion. "I'm afraid he has paid dearly for his kindness of heart!"

"Solon," said Mr. Dinsmore, "mount the fastest horse here and ride to Roselands for Dr. Arthur. Tell him we don't know how seriously this gentleman is hurt. Hurry! Make all possible haste!"

Solon was turning to obey, but stopped, exclaiming, "Why sho' anuff, dar's de doctah hisself just ligtin' off his hoss ober yondah!"

"Then run and bring him here."

Arthur obeyed the summons with all speed. The alarm of the fire had reached Roselands, and he had hastened to the spot to give aid in extinguishing it, or to any who might be injured.

He found the captain showing signs of life. He moved his head, then opened his eyes.

"Where are you hurt, sir?" asked the doctor.

"Not very seriously anywhere, I trust," replied the captain, trying to rise. "Ah!" as he fell back again, "both back and ankle seem to have had a wrench. But, friends, are you not needed over there at the fire? My injuries can wait."

"Little or nothing more can be done there, and there are people enough on the ground now to leave us free to attend to you," said Mr. Dinsmore.

The doctor was speaking aside to Donald and Solon. Coming back, "We will have a litter ready in a few moment," he said, "and carry you over to Ion."

"By all means," said Mr. Dinsmore. "You accompany us, of course, Arthur?"

"Certainly, sir."

"How is she — the old Negress? Was she much injured by the fall?" Captain Raymond asked.

No one could tell him, and he begged the doctor to attend to her while the litter was being prepared.

Arthur went in search of her, and presently returned saying she had escaped without any broken bones, though apparently a good deal shaken up and bruised.

CHAPTER IX

Man proposes, but God disposes.

DONALD LEFT ION the next morning, going away sadly and alone, yet trying to be truly thankful that his friend's injuries, though severe, were not permanent, and that he left him where he would have the best of medical treatment and nursing.

"Don't be uneasy about the captain," Mr. Dinsmore said in parting. "I can assure you that Arthur is a skillful physician and surgeon, and we have several Negro women who thoroughly understand nursing. Besides, my wife, Elsie and I will oversee them and do all in our power for the comfort and restoration of the invalid."

"Thank you, cousin. I am sure nothing will be left undone that skill and kindness can do," Donald said, shaking with warmth the hand Mr. Dinsmore held out to him. "Raymond is one in a thousand. I've known him for years, and he has been a good and valuable friend to me. I wish it were possible for me to stay and wait on him myself; but army men are not their own masters, you know. He'll be wanting to get back to his ship before he's able. Don't let him."

"Not if I can prevent it," was Mr. Dinsmore's laughing rejoinder. "By the way, should not some word be sent to his wife?"

"Wife! She has been dead for some two years, I think. I asked him if there was any relative he would wish informed of his condition, and he said no. His parents are not living, he has neither brother nor sister, and his children were too young to be troubled about it."

"Poor fellow!" exclaimed Mr. Dinsmore, thinking of his own happier lot — the sweet wife and daughter at Ion, the other daughter and son, father, sisters, grandchildren and nephews who would flock about him in tender solicitude, were he laid low by sickness or accident.

Leaving Donald in the city, he drove back to Ion full of sympathy for his injured guest and admiration for his courage and fortitude. He had made no moan or complaint, though evidently suffering great pain and much solicitude on account of the long prospective detention from official duty.

The doctor's verdict was a week or more in bed, probably six weeks before the ankle could be used.

"You must get me up much sooner than that, doctor, if it be a possible thing," Captain Raymond said most emphatically.

"I can only promise to do my best," was Arthur's response. "Nature must have time for her work of recuperation."

Elsie met her father in the entrance hall on his return. "Ah, papa," she said, looking up smilingly into his face, "I think you will have to rescind your order."

"In regard to what?" he asked, stopping to lay a hand lightly on he shoulder, while he smoothed her hair caressingly with the other.

"The week of entire rest you bade me take."

"No, there is to be no recall of that order."

"But our poor injured guest, father? Injured in the noble effort to save the life of another!"

"He shall have every care and attention without any assistance from you, or Rose either — at least for the present."

"But, dear papa, to have you worn out and made ill would be worse than anything else."

"That does not follow as an inevitable consequence, and you may safely trust me to take excellent care of number one," he said with playful look and tone.

"Ah, papa, there is not the least use in your trying to make me believe there is any selfishness in you!"

"No, I presume not. You have always been persistently blind to my many imperfections. Well, daughter, you need not be troubled lest I should waste too much strength on the poor captain. I do not imagine him to be an exacting person, and we have enough efficient nurses among the servants to do all the work that is needful. My part will be, I think, principally to cheer him, keep up his spirits, and see that he is provided with everything that can contribute to comfort of mind and body. I must leave you now and go to him. I advise a drive for you and your mamma as soon as you can make ready for it — the air is delightfully clear and bracing."

"Thank you, papa. The advice shall be followed immediately so far as I am concerned, and the order carefully obeyed," she answered as he moved on down the hall.

The smile with which the captain greeted Mr. Dinsmore's entrance into the room where he lay in pain and despondency was a rather melancholy one.

"My dear sir, I feel for you!" Mr. Dinsmore said, seating himself by the bedside, "but you are a brave man and a Christian, and can endure hardness as a good soldier of Jesus Christ."

There was a flash of joy in the sufferer's eyes as he turned them upon the speaker. "That, sir, is the most comforting and sustaining thing you could have said to me!" Through what suffering was the Captain of our salvation made perfect! And shall I shrink from enduring a little in His service? Ah no! And when I reflect that I might have been killed, and my children left fatherless, I feel that I have room for nothing but thankfulness that it is as well with me as it is."

"And that some good will be brought out of this trial we cannot doubt," Mr. Dinsmore said. "For 'we know that all things work together for good to them that love God, to them who are the called according to His purpose.'"

"Yes, and 'I reckon that the sufferings of this present time are not worthy to be compared with the glory which shall be revealed in us.' 'We glory in tribulation also, knowing that tribulation worketh patience, and patience experience, and experience hope, and hope making not ashamed; because the love of God is shed abroad in our hearts by the Holy Ghost which is given unto us.' "

"What a wonderful book the Bible is!" remarked Mr. Dinsmore meditatively. "What stores of comfort and encouragement it contains for all in whatever state or condition! 'The law of thy mouth is better unto me than thousands of gold and silver.' "

"Yes, how true it is, Mr. Dinsmore, that 'it is not in man that walketh to direct his steps'! I had fully resolved to return today to my vessel, and now when may I hope to see her? Not in less than six weeks, the doctor tells me."

"A weary while it must seem in prospect. But we will do all we can to make it short in passing and prevent you from regretting the necessity of tarrying with us for so much longer time than you had intended," Mr. Dinsmore answered in a cheery tone.

"Your great kindness is laying me under lasting obligations, Mr. Dinsmore," the captain responded with glistening eyes, "obligations which I shall never, I fear, have an opportunity to repay."

"My dear sir. I am truly thankful to have it in my power to do what can be done to alleviate your sufferings and restore the health and vigor you so nobly sacrificed for another. Besides, what Christian can recall the Master's assurance that He will consider any kindness done to any follower of His as done to Himself, and not rejoice in the opportunity to be of service to a fellow disciple, be it man, woman, or child?"

"Yes, 'and the King shall answer and say unto them, Verily I say unto you, inasmuch as ye have done it unto the least of these my brethren, ye have done it unto me.' "

"Ah, captain, don't talk of obligation to one who has a recompense such as that in view!" Mr. Dinsmore said, a smile on his lip, a glad light in his eye.

The captain stretched out his hand and grasped that of his host. "What cause for gratitude that I have fallen into the care of those who can appreciate and act from such motives!" he exclaimed with emotion.

"You are the hero of the hour, my friend," Mr. Dinsmore

remarked after a short silence. "I wish you could have seen the faces of my wife, daughter, and granddaughter when they heard of the noble, unselfish, and courageous deed which was the cause of your sore injuries."

"Don't mention it!" exclaimed the captain, a manly flush suffusing his face. "Who could stand by and see a fellow creature perish without so much as stretching out a helping hand?"

In the weeks that followed, Captain Raymond won golden opinions from those with whom he sojourned, showing himself as capable of the courage of endurance as of that more ordinary kind that incites to deeds of daring. He was always patient and cheerful, and sufficiently at leisure from himself and his own troubles to show a keen interest in those about him.

After the first week, he was able to take possession of an invalid-chair, which was then wheeled into the room where the family was wont to gather for the free and unrestrained enjoyment of each other's company.

They made him one of themselves and he found it a rare treat to be among them thus day after day, getting such an insight into their domestic life and true character as years of ordinary exchanges would not have given him. He learned to love them all — the kind, cheerful, unselfish older people; the sweet-faced, gentle, tender mother; the fair and lovely maiden, lovely in mind and person; the brave, frank, open-hearted lads; and the dear, innocent little ones.

He studied them all furtively and with increasing interest, growing more and more reconciled the while to his involuntary detention among them.

Oftentimes they were all there, but occasionally one of the grandparents or the mother would be away at Roselands for a day or two, taking turns in ministering to Mrs. Conly, and comforting and cheering her feeble old father.

"You have no idea, my dear sir," the captain one day remarked to his host, "how delightful it is to a man who has passed most of his life on shipboard, away from women and children, to be taken into such a family circle as this! I think you who live in it a highly favored man, sir!"

"I quite agree with you," Mr. Dinsmore said. "I think we are an exceptionally happy family, though not exempt from the trials incident to life in this world of sin and sorrow."

"Your daughter is an admirable mother," the captain went on, "so gentle and affectionate, and yet so firm. Her children show by their behavior that their training has been very nearly if not quite faultless. And in seeing so much of them I realize as never before the hardship of the constant separation from my own which my profession entails. I ask myself, 'If I were with them thus day after day, should I find them as obedient, docile, and intelligent as these little ones? Will my Max be as fine a lad as Harold or Herbert? Can I hope to see Lulu and Gracie grow up into such lovely maidenhood as that of Miss Violet?' "

"I sincerely hope you may be so blessed, captain," Mr. Dinsmore said, "but much will depend upon the training to which they are subjected. There is truth in the old proverb, 'Just as the twig is bent the tree's inclined.' "

"Yes, sir, and a higher authority says, 'Train up a child in the way he should go, and when he is old he will not depart from it.' But my difficulty is that I can neither train them myself, nor see that the work is rightly done by others."

"That is sad, indeed," Mr. Dinsmore replied with sincere sympathy. "But, my dear sir, is there not strong consolation in the thought that you can pray for them, and that 'the effectual fervent prayer of a righteous man availeth much'?"

"There is indeed, sir!" the captain said with emotion. "And also in the promise, 'I will establish my covenant between me and thee, and thy seed after thee in their generations, for an everlasting covenant, to be a God unto thee, and to thy seed after thee.' "

CHAPTER X

One Pinch, hungry, leanfac'd villain.

—SHAKESPEARE

CAPTAIN RAYMOND'S two little daughters were at this time in a village in one of the northern states, in charge of Mrs. Beulah Scrimp, a distant relative on the mother's side.

Mrs. Scrimp was a widow living in a rather genteel style in a house and upon means left her by her late husband. She was a managing woman, fond of money; therefore, glad of the increase to her income yielded by the liberal sum Captain Raymond had offered her as compensation for the board and care of his motherless little girls.

She had undertaken Max also at first, but given him up as beyond her control. And now, though continuing to attend school in town, he boarded with the Rev. Thomas Fox, who lived upon its outskirts.

Mrs. Scrimp was a woman of economies, keeping vigilant watch over all expenditures, great and small. She employed one servant only, who was cook, housemaid and laundress all in one, and expected to give every moment of her time to the service of her mistress, and be content with smaller wages than many who did less work.

Mrs. Scrimp was a woman of theories also, and her pet one accorded well with the aforementioned characteristic. It was that two meals a day were sufficient for anyone, and that none but the very vigorous and hard working ought to eat anything between three o'clock in the afternoon and breakfast the next morning.

That was a rule to which neither Max nor Lulu could ever be made to submit. But Grace, the youngest, was a delicate, fragile child with little force of will. She had no strength or power to resist, so fell victim to the theory. Each night she went supperless to bed, and each day found herself too feeble and languid to take part in the active sports in which her stronger sister delighted.

It is quite possible that Mrs. Scrimp had no intention of being cruel, but merely made the not uncommon mistake of supposing that what is good for one person is of course good for everybody else. She was dyspeptic and insisted that she found her favorite plan exceedingly beneficial in her own case; therefore, she was sure so delicate a child as Gracie ought to conform to the same regimen.

She seemed fond of the little girl, petted and caressed her, calling her by many an endearing name, and telling her very often that she was "a good, docile child — far better than fiery-tempered, headstrong Lulu."

Lulu would hear the remark with a scornful smile and toss of the head, sometimes saying proudly, "I wouldn't let anybody call you names to me, Gracie; and I wouldn't be such a little goose as to be wheedled and flattered into putting up with being half-starved."

There had been a time when Mrs. Scrimp tried to prevent and punish such daring words, but she had given up long since and contented herself with sighing sadly over the "depravity of that irrepressible child."

She had once or twice threatened to write to Captain Raymond and tell him that Lulu was unmanageable, but the child coolly replied, "I wish you would. Then papa would send Gracie and me somewhere else to stay."

"Where you would, perhaps, fare a deal worse," returned Mrs. Scrimp wrathfully.

"I am willing to risk it," Lulu said, and that was the end of it, for Mrs. Scrimp would have been very loath to lose the children's board.

One pleasant October morning Lulu came down a trifle late to her breakfast. Mrs. Scrimp and Gracie were already seated at the table and had begun their meal.

"Lulu," said Mrs. Scrimp with a portentous frown, "you were in the pantry last night, helping yourself."

"Of course I was," returned the child as she took her seat at the table. "I told you I wouldn't go without my supper, and you didn't have Ann get any for me, so what could I do but help myself?"

"You have no right to go into my pantry and take food that belongs to me. It's neither more nor less than stealing, Miss Lulu Raymond."

"Well, Aunt Beulah, what do you call it when you take money my father pays you for feeding Gracie and me, and don't give us the food he has paid for?"

Mrs. Scrimp colored violently at that, but quickly answered, "He doesn't pay for any particular kind or quantity, and doesn't want you overfed. And I don't consider it at all good for you to eat after three o'clock, as I've told you fifty times."

"Oftener than that, I dare say," returned Lulu with indifference, "but you might say it five hundred times and I shouldn't believe it a bit more. Papa and mamma never had us put to bed without our supper. They always gave us plenty to eat whenever we were hungry, and Gracie was far stronger than she is now."

Mrs. Scrimp was exasperated into a return to old tactics. "Lulu, you are the most impudent child I ever saw!" she exclaimed. "You shall go without supper tonight, if it were only to punish you for talking as you have this morning."

"No, I'll not. I'll have something to eat if I must go to the neighbors for it."

"I'll lock you up."

"Then I'll call out to the people in the street and tell them you won't give me enough to eat. And just as soon as papa comes, I'll tell him all about it right before you."

"You wouldn't dare tell him how you've talked to me; he'd punish you for your impertinence."

"No, he would say it was justifiable under the circumstances."

"Dear me!" sighed Mrs. Scrimp, lifting hands and eyes in holy horror, "what a time your stepmother will have with you! I shouldn't want to be in her place."

"My stepmother!" cried Lulu, growing very red, while her dark eyes flashed with anger. "I haven't any! What do you mean by talking in that way, Aunt Beulah?"

Mrs. Scrimp's laugh jarred very unpleasantly upon the nerves of the excited child.

"Your father will be presenting you with one some of these days, I'll warrant," she said in a tantalizing tone.

Lulu felt ready to burst into passionate weeping, but would not give her tormentor the satisfaction of seeing her do so. She struggled determinedly with her emotions, and presently was able to say in a tone of perfect indifference, "Well, I don't care if he does, anything will be better than staying here with you."

"Ungrateful, hateful child!" said Mrs. Scrimp. "Gracie's a real comfort to me, but you are just the opposite."

"Aunt Beulah," said Lulu, fixing her keen eyes steadily upon Mrs. Scrimp's face, "you've called me ungrateful ever so many times. Now I'd like to know what I have to be grateful for toward you? My father pays you well for everything you do for Gracie and me."

"There are some things that can't be bought with money, and that money can't pay for, Miss Impertinence," said Mrs. Scrimp, and having satisfied her appetite, rose from the table and, taking Gracie by the hand, walked out of the room with her in the most dignified manner.

Presently afterward Lulu saw her, through the window, in bonnet and shawl and with a basket on her arm, going out to do the marketing.

Having finished her breakfast, Lulu walked into the sitting room.

Gracie lay on the sofa looking pale and weak. Lulu went to her, stroked her hair and kissed her.

"Poor little Gracie! Weren't you hungry for some supper last night?"

"Yes, Lulu," replied the child, lifting a thin white little

hand and stroking her sister's face, "but Aunt Beulah says it makes me worse to eat at night."

"I don't believe it!" cried Lulu vehemently, and half stamping her foot. "I'm going to write a letter to papa and tell him how she starves you, and would starve me too if I'd let her!"

"I wish papa would come!" sighed Gracie. "Lulu, did it use to make us sick to eat supper when we lived with papa and mamma?"

"No, never a bit! Oh, Gracie, Gracie, why did mamma die? Why did God take her away from us when we need her so much? I can't love Him for that! I don't love Him!" she exclaimed with a sudden shower of tears, albeit not much given to shedding them.

"Don't cry, Lulu," Gracie said in distress, "maybe papa will find another mamma for us. I wish he would."

"I don't! Stepmothers are always hateful! I'd hate her and never mind a word she said. Oh, Max, Max! I'm so glad to see you!" as a handsome, dark-eyed, merry-faced boy came rushing in.

"I've just come for a minute!" he cried half breathlessly, catching her in his arms, giving her a resounding kiss, then bending over Gracie with a sudden change to extreme gentleness of manner. She was his baby sister and so weak and timid.

"Poor little Gracie!" he said softly. "I wish I was a big man to take you and Lulu away and give you a good time!"

"I love you, Max," she returned, stroking and patting his cheek. "I wish you'd be a good boy, so you could live here with us."

"I don't want to," he answered, frowning. "I mean I don't want to live with her. I sha'n't ever call her aunt again. I wouldn't have come in if I hadn't known she was out. I saw her going to the market. I'm off to Miller's Pond to fish for trout. You know it's Saturday and there's no school. Jim Bates is going with me and we're to be back by noon; that is, old Tommy said I must."

Lulu laughed at Max's irreverent manner of alluding to the man who had oversight of him out of school hours.

Then, jumping up, "Oh, Max!' she cried, "I want to go too! I'll be ready in a minute."

"What'll Mrs. Scrimp say?" laughed Max.

Lulu tossed her head with a scornful smile that said more plainly than words that she did not care what Mrs. Scrimp might do or say in regard to the matter, ran into the hall, and returned almost immediately with hat and coat.

"Come, Max," she said, "we'd better be off before she gets back. Gracie, you won't mind being left alone for just a little bit? Ann's in the kitchen, you know."

"I wish I could go too!" sighed Gracie. "I wish I could run about and have good times like you and Max!"

"Maybe you will, some of these days. Goodbye, little one," said Max, giving a parting pat to the little white cheek.

"Goodbye," cried Lulu from the doorway. "Don't fret, because maybe I'll find something pretty to bring you when I come back."

She took a small basket from the table in the hall, Max shouldered his fishing rod that he had left there behind the front door, and they went out together.

CHAPTER XI

*Bear a fair presence, though your heart be tainted,
Teach sin the carriage of a holy saint.*

—SHAKESPEARE

THE CHILDREN WALKED VERY FAST, glancing this way and that till satisfied that there was no longer any danger of encountering Mrs. Scrimp, then their pace slackened a little and they breathed more freely.

"Won't she be mad because you came without asking her, Lu?" queried Max.

"I s'pose so."

"What'll she do about it?"

"Scold, scold, scold! And threaten to make me fast. But she knows she can't do that. I always manage to get something to eat. I've found a key that fits the pantry door, so I just help myself. She doesn't know about the key and wonders how it happens — thinks she forgot to lock it."

"But, Lulu, you wouldn't steal?"

"'Tain't stealing to take what papa pays for! Max you're too stupid!" cried Lulu indignantly.

Max gave a long, low whistle. "Fact, Lu! That's so! Our father does pay for more than we can possibly eat, and expects us to have all we want."

"Do you get enough, Max?"

"Yes, and right good, too. Mrs. Fox is real good and kind. But he's just awful! I tell you, Lu, if I don't thrash him within an inch of his life when I grow to be a man, it'll be strange."

"Tell me about him. What does he do to you?"

"Well, in the first place, he pretends to be very good

and pious. He preaches and prays and talks to me as if I were the greatest sinner in the world, while all the time he's ten times worse himself and the biggest kind of hypocrite. He tells me it's very wicked when I get angry at his hateful treatment of me, and gets mad as a March hare himself while he's talking about it."

"Well, I'd let him storm and never care a cent."

"Yes, but that isn't all. He beats me dreadfully for the least little thing, and sometimes for nothing at all. One time, he bought a new padlock for the barn door and pretty soon it disappeared. He couldn't find it anywhere, so he called me and asked me what I had done with it. I said I hadn't touched it, hadn't seen it, didn't even know he had bought one. That was the truth. But he wouldn't believe me; he said I must have taken it, for I was the only mischievous person about the place, and if I didn't own up and show him where it was, he'd horsewhip me till I did."

"Oh, Max! The wicked old wretch!" cried Lulu, between clenched teeth. "What did you do? You couldn't tell a lie!"

"No, I thought I couldn't, Lu; and I'm so ashamed!" said Max, growing red and tears starting to his eyes. "But he beat me, and beat me, and beat me till I thought he'd kill me. And so to stop him, at last I said I took it. But I didn't gain anything, for of course he asked next where it was, and I couldn't tell him because I didn't know. So he began again; but I fainted, and I suppose that scared him and made him stop. He didn't say anything more about the padlock till weeks afterward it was found in the hay and it was clear I didn't have anything to do with it."

"Oh, that old wretch!" cried Lulu again. "Didn't he tell you then he was sorry for having abused you so when you were innocent?"

"No, indeed! Not him! He said, 'Well, you didn't deserve it that time, but I've no doubt you've escaped many a time when you did!'"

"Max, I'd never stand it! I'd run away!" exclaimed

Lulu, stopping short and facing her brother with eyes that fairly blazed with indignation.

"I've thought of that, Lu. I've felt tempted to do it more than once," Max said with a sigh, "but I thought how papa would feel hearing of it. I'd rather bear it all than have him feel that his son had done anything to disgrace him."

"Max, you're better than I am!" cried Lulu with affectionate warmth. "I'd never have thought of anything but how to get away as fast as possible from that horrid, horrid beast of a man."

"Papa thinks he's good, and that's the reason he put me with him. Oh, but don't I wish he knew the truth!"

"I should think the old rascal would be afraid of what papa may do when he comes and hears all the things you'll have to tell."

"I suppose he thinks papa will believe his story instead of mine; and perhaps he will," said Max a little sadly.

"No, don't you be one bit afraid of that!" cried Lulu hotly. "Papa knows you're a truthful boy. His children couldn't be liars!"

"But you know I can't say any more than I've never told an untruth," said Max, coloring painfully.

"Well, you couldn't help it." Lulu said, trying to comfort him. "I'm afraid that I might have done it myself to keep from being killed."

"Hello! Here comes Jim!" cried Max with a sudden change of tone, his face brightening wonderfully as a lad somewhat older in appearance than\ himself, and carrying a fishing rod over his shoulder, came hurrying down a lane and joined them.

"Hello, Max," he said, "we've a splendid day for fishing, haven't we?" Then in a whisper, "Who's this you're taking along?"

"My sister Lulu," Max answered aloud. "She'll help us dig worms for bait, won't you, Lu?"

"Yes, if you'll let me fish a little after you've caught some."

"Good morning, Miss Lulu," said Jim, lifting his hat.

"Good morning," she returned, giving him a careless nod.

"It's a long walk for a girl," he remarked.

"Oh," said Max laughing, "she's half boy; ain't you, Lu?"

"I s'pose, if you mean in walking, jumping and running. Aunt Beulah calls me a regular tomboy. But I'd rather be that than stay cooped up in the house all the time."

They had now left the town behind, and presently they turned from the highway and took a narrow path that led them deep into the woods, now in the very height of its autumnal beauty.

The sun shone brightly, but through a mellow haze; the air was deliciously pure, cool and bracing.

The children's pulses bounded, they laughed and jested. The boys whistled and Lulu sang in a voice of birdlike melody.

"Oh, Max," she said, "I wish Gracie was well and with us here!"

"Yes, so do I," he answered, "but 'tisn't likely she can ever be strong like you and me, Lu."

"Well, I'll tell her all about it and take her all the pretty things I can find. Oh, what a lovely place!" she said as they came out upon the shore of the pond, a tiny sheet of clear still water surrounded by woods and hills except where a rivulet entered it on one side and left it on the other.

"Yes," assented Jim, "it's a right nice place, is Miller's Pond, and has lots of nice fish in it."

The boys laid down their rods, Lulu her basket, and all three fell to digging for earthworms.

When they deemed that they had a sufficient quantity of bait, the lads seated themselves on the roots of a fallen tree close to the water, each with fishing rod in hand, and Lulu, picking up her basket, wandered off among the trees and bushes.

"Don't go too far away and get lost," Max called after her.

"No," she answered, "I'll not go out of sight of the pond, so I can easily find my way back. But don't you go off and leave me."

"No, if you're not here, I'll hallo when we're 'most ready to start."

What treasures Lulu found as she wandered here and there, every now and then turning to look for the pond, and make sure that she was not losing herself. There were acorn cups, lovely mosses, beautiful autumn leaves — red, orange, golden and green. There were wild grapes, too, and hazelnuts, brown and ripe. Of all these she gathered eagerly until her basket was full, thinking that some would delight Gracie, others appease Aunt Beulah.

And now she made her way back to the spot where the boys still sat, each with his line in the water.

"Have you caught any?" she asked.

"Yes," said Max, "I've caught six and Jim has eight. There! I've got another!" he shouted, giving his line a jerk that sent a pretty speckled trout floundering in the grass.

"I'll take it off the hook for you," said Lulu, springing forward and dropping on her knees beside it. "And then you'll let me try, won't you?"

"Yes," Max answered in a half reluctant tone, getting up to give her his place.

"There are hazelnuts right over there a little way," Lulu said, pointing with her finger.

"Oh, then I'll have some!" cried Max, stating on a run in the direction indicated.

He came back after a little while bringing some in his hat, picked up some stones, and seating himself near the others, cracked his nuts, sharing generously with them.

Presently Lulu had her first bite, succeeded in bringing her prize safely to land, and was quite wild with delight.

Max rejoiced with her, taking brotherly pride in her success.

"You'll do for a fisherman or fisherwoman," he said happily. "I sha'n't be much surprised if you beat me at it one o' these days."

Then struck with a sudden unwelcome thought, "I wonder what time it is!" He jumped up from the ground in haste and perturbation. "Do you s'pose it's noon yet, Jim?"

"Which way's the sun?" queried the latter, glancing toward the sky. "It ought to be right overhead at noon. Why it's down some toward the west! I shouldn't wonder if it's as late as two o'clock."

"Two o'clock!" cried Max in dismay, "and I was to be back by noon! Won't I catch it!" and he began gathering up his fish and fishing tackle in great haste, Jim doing likewise, with the remark that he would be late to dinner and maybe have to go without.

Lulu was giving Max all the assistance in her power, her face full of sympathy.

"Max," she whispered, hurrying along close at his side as they started on their homeward way, "don't let that horrid, cruel, wicked man beat you! I wouldn't. I'd fight him like anything!"

Max shook his head. "'Twouldn't do any good, Lulu. He's so much bigger and stronger than I am that fighting him would be worse for me than taking the thrashing quietly."

"I could never do that!" she said. "But don't wait for me if you want to go faster."

"I don't," said Max.

"Well, I b'lieve I'd better make all the haste I can," said Jim. "So, goodbye," and away he sped.

"Oh, if papa only knew all about how that brute treats you!" sighed Lulu.

"Max, can't we write him a letter?"

"I do once in a while, but old Tom always reads it before it goes."

"I wouldn't let him. I'd hide away somewhere to write it, and put it in the post office myself."

"I have no chance. He gives me only a sheet of paper at a time, and must always know what I do with it. It's the same way my pocket money, so I can't buy postage stamps. And I don't know how to direct the letter, either."

"Oh, dear! And it's the same way with me!" sighed Lulu. "When will papa come? I'm just sick to see him and tell him everything!"

When they reached Mrs. Scrimp's door, Max gave Lulu his string of fish, saying, "Here, take them, Sis. It's no use for me to keep 'em, for I shouldn't get a taste; and maybe they'll put her in a good humor with you."

"Thank you," she said. "Oh, Max, I wish you could eat them yourself!" Her eyes were full of tears.

"I'd rather you'd have 'em — you and Gracie," he said cheerfully. "Goodbye."

"Goodbye," she returned, looking after him as he hurried away, whistling as he went.

"He's whistling to keep his courage up. Oh, Max! Poor Max! I wish I could give that man the worst kind of flogging!" Lulu sighed to herself, then turned and went into the house.

She heard Mrs. Scrimp's voice in the kitchen scolding Ann for letting the bread burn in the oven. It was an inauspicious moment to appear before her, but Lulu marched boldly in, holding up her string of fish.

"See Aunt Beulah! They're just fresh out of the water, and won't they make us a nice dinner?"

"And they're your favorite fish, ma'am, them pretty speckled trout is," put in Ann, glad to make a diversion in her own favor, as well as to help Lulu out of a scrape. "I'll go right to work to clean 'em and have 'em ready for the frying pan in less than no time."

"Yes, they'll be very nice, and the meat will keep for tomorrow," was the gracious rejoinder. "You oughtn't to have gone off without leave, Lulu; but I suppose Max couldn't wait."

"No, Aunt Beulah, he said he couldn't stay more than a minute. Shall I help Ann clean the fish?"

"No, go and make yourself tidy. Your hands are dirty, your apron soiled, and your hair looks as if it hadn't been combed for a week."

Mrs. Scrimp's face was gathering blackness as she scanned the figure of the young delinquent from head to foot, spying out all that was amiss with it.

"I will," said Lulu, moving toward the door with cheerful alacrity. "Oh, I forgot!" and rushing into the hall, she came back the next minute bringing her basket of treasures.

"See, Aunt Beulah, I've brought you lots of lovely leaves. You know you said you wanted some to make a wreath. And here are some mosses, and grapes, and hazelnuts."

"Why you have made good use of your time," Mrs. Scrimp said, now entirely mollified. "Bring your basket into the sitting room where Gracie is and we'll look over it's contents."

Max was less fortunate today than his sister. His custodian was on the look out for him, cowhide in hand, and seizing him roughly, as he entered the gate, with a fierce, "I'll teach you to disobey orders another time, you young vagabond! I told you to come home at noon, and you're over two hours behind time!" began administering an unmerciful flogging.

"Stop!" cried Max, trying to dodge the blows. "How can I tell the time? I came as soon as I thought it was noon."

But his tormentor was in a towering passion and would not stay his hand to listen to any excuse.

"Do you mean to kill me?" screamed Max. "You'll hang for it if you do. And my father —."

"Your father believes in enforcing obedience to orders, sir; and I'll —."

But at this instant there was an interference from a third party.

At a little distance some men were at work hewing timber. They had been working there for weeks, in which Max had made their acquaintance and become a great favorite with them, particularly one called by his companions "Big Bill," because of his great size and strength.

He was a rough, good-natured man, with nothing of the bully about him, but regarded with intense scorn and indignation any attempt on the part of the strong to tyrannize over the weak and defenseless.

He and his comrades had seen and heard enough in these weeks of labor in the vicinity of Fox's residence to inspire them with contempt and dislike toward him on account of his treatment of Max. They had among themselves already pronounced him "a wolf in sheep's clothing, a hypocrite and a coward."

They had seen him watching for the boy with his instrument of torture in his hand, and their wrath was waxed hot.

When Max came in sight they dropped their tools and looked to see what would happen, and at the first blow "Big Bill" muttering between his clenched teeth, "I'll settle his hash for him," started for the scene of action. "Stop that!" he roared, "stop that, you old hypocritical scoundrel! You hit that boy another lick and I'll knock you as flat as a flounder!"

The hand that held the whip dropped at Fox's side, and the other loosed its hold on Max as he turned and faced his assailant.

"What do you mean by coming here to interfere in my business?" he demanded.

"I mean to protect the weak against the strong, sir. I consider that my business. You've given that boy more unmerciful beatings already than he ought to have had in a lifetime, and he's not at all a bad boy either. I know all about that padlock affair, though he's never breathed a word to me on the subject, and I'd enjoy nothing better than thrashing you soundly. What's more, I'll do it if ever I know you to strike him again, or my names not Bill Simpson. Max, if he ever does, you've only to let "Big Bill" hear of it and he'll get ten times more than he's given."

"Thank you, Bill," said Max, running to the big, kind-hearted fellow and giving him his hand. "I'm glad to be protected from him, though I don't want him hurt if he'll only let me alone."

Fox had already stalked away in the direction of the house, swelling with inward wrath, but assuming an air of injured innocence and offended dignity.

Standing in wholesome fear of Max's self-constituted defender, he never again ventured to lay violent hands on the lad, but contented himself with inflicting many petty annoyances.

CHAPTER XII

Except I be by Silvia in the night,
There is no music in the nightingale;
Unless I look on Silvia in the day,
There is no day for me to look upon.

— SHAKESPEARE

IT WAS ALREADY PAST the middle of November when Captain Raymond received his injuries, so that the six weeks or more of enforced inaction would carry him into the month of January.

He had hoped to spend Christmas with his children, but that was now clearly impossible, as he sadly owned to himself, for he was a loving father and felt the disappointment keenly on both his own account and theirs.

There would be no festivities at Ion this year, bereavement was still too recent with themselves, too imminent with those very near by the ties of kindred. But there was to be an exchange of gifts; there had been that even last year when but a few months had elapsed since the departure to the better land of the beloved husband and father.

Captain Raymond, sitting quietly in his invalid chair, generally to all appearance buried in a book, overheard many a consultation in regard to what would be most acceptable to this or that one who happened to be absent from the room at the moment. It was intended that most of the gifts, at least, should be surprises to the recipients.

One day when the talk was of those to be provided for Rosie and Walter, Mrs. Dinsmore noticed that their guest was listening with a very interested look.

"Captain Raymond," she said, turning to him with

an engaging smile, "we purpose to go into the city tomorrow to shop for these things; can we do anything in that line for you?"

"Thank you," he said heartily, his face brightening very much. "If it would not be overtaxing you, I should be very glad to have the benefit of your and Mrs. Travilla's taste and judgement in the selection of some Christmas presents for my children. It will be all I can do for them this year. I had thought of sending money for the purpose to the persons in charge of them, but it would be far more satisfactory to me to have some share in the choice of the articles."

Both ladies assured him that it would give them pleasure to do whatever they could to assist him in making the desired purchases, and Mr. Dinsmore suggested that a variety of goods might be sent out from the city stores for him to select from.

He said that was a good idea, but he would leave it to the ladies to have that done, or to choose for him a book for each of his children, a doll for each girl, and writing desks, fully furnished, for Max and Lulu.

"I think," he added with a smile, "whatever I may give will seem to them more valuable if sent from a distance than if bought near at hand."

"Yes," Mrs. Dinsmore said, "that is human nature."

The shoppers set out the next morning soon after breakfast, expecting to return about the usual dinner hour.

Watching the departure from the window near which he was seated, the captain observed with pleasure that Violet was not of the party, hoping that if left behind, she would give him the enjoyment of her company during the absence of the others.

Presently she came in, bringing some needlework. Rosie and Walter were with her.

The captain closed the book he had been reading and turned toward them with a pleased smile.

"So I am not to be left to solitude, as I feared," he remarked.

"You must please send us away, sir, whenever you think that preferable to our company," returned Violet lightly.

"Do you deem me capable of such rudeness, Miss Travilla?" he asked with playful look and tone.

"We will not consider it such," she answered, seating herself and beginning her work, "since we can wander at will all over the house, while, for the present, you, sir, are a prisoner confined to this room and the next."

"That reminds me," he said, "that of late you have absented yourself a great deal from this room, to my small discontent."

"It is flattering to my vanity and self-appreciation to learn that you have missed me," she returned sportively, but with a slightly heightened color.

"You can never be away from the rest of us without being missed, Vi," remarked Rosie, "especially now that Sister Elsie is away."

"And do you not mean to gratify my curiosity as to what has been the cause of your many and prolonged absences, Miss Violet?" queried the captain.

"I have been busy elsewhere, sir. But is it not an understood thing that curiosity is a peculiarly feminine trait?"

"I am able to plead guiltless to the charge of ever having made such an insinuation," said the captain, "and do now confess to having a full share of inquisitiveness."

"May I tell, Vi?" asked Rosie.

"We must first learn whether Captain Raymond can keep a secret," Vi answered, glancing at him with a saucy smile.

"Yes, indeed!" he said, "as you shall learn if you will but allow me the opportunity."

"Then I may tell!" cried Rosie, and hardly waiting for her sister's nod of acquiescence, went on. "She is preparing such a nice surprise for dear mamma, Captain Raymond, a miniature of papa which she has been painting on ivory. I think it looks more like him than any photograph or painted portrait that we have. And I am sure mamma could not have a more acceptable present.

Besides that, Vi has painted two flower pieces — one for grandpa and one for grandma."

"You have certainly been very industrious, Miss Violet," he remarked. "I have heard your studio spoken of. May I hope for the pleasure of visiting it when I recover the free use of my limbs?"

"That will not be for some weeks, sir, and in the meanwhile I will take your request into consideration," she answered demurely.

The morning passed very rapidly for the captain. The children amused him with their prattle, and when after an hour or two, Rosie grew tired of the bit of fancywork she was doing under her sister's supervision and yielded to Walter's entreaties to "come to the nursery and build block houses," it left Violet his sole companion. The moments sped faster than before, for he found her a very interesting and entertaining conversationalist.

On their return, the shopping party brought with them the articles he had mentioned. He pronounced them all entirely satisfactory, and they were packed and sent northward with the addition of some pretty things for the dolls, contributed by Violet and Rosie.

Some unusual impulse of fatherly solicitude and affection led the captain to put his own address upon several envelopes in each writing desk, stamping them also, and adding a note to each of the three children. To Man and Lulu he said that he wanted letters from them which should not pass through the hands of a third person, "letters that should be like bit of private chat with papa."

Seeing how tenderly and carefully the little Travillas were nurtured and what love was lavished upon them, had turned his thoughts frequently upon his own motherless ones, and set him to thinking and asking himself rather anxiously how they were faring in those respects. He had come to realize more thoroughly than ever before his responsibility as a parent.

The Christmas work which had kept Violet busy in her studio was now finished. Henceforth she spent much more of her time with the rest of the family, greatly to Captain Raymond's satisfaction. For much as he admired the other ladies and enjoyed conversing with them and with Mr. Dinsmore, he was quite conscious of a constant uneasiness and discontent when Violet absented herself from the room.

His admiration for her beauty and grace had been unbounded from the first, and gradually as he discovered more and more of her sterling worth — her sweetness and unselfishness of disposition, her talent, industry and genuine piety — his heart had gone out to her in ardent affection, in fact with a deeper and stronger love than he had ever before known or dreamed of.

He began to ask himself how he could ever go away and leave her, and whether he dared seek to make her his own. He was fully as loath as Donald Keith to appear in the role of fortune hunter. Would Mr. Dinsmore and his daughter, so noble themselves, be ready to impute so unworthy a motive to him? He hoped not; he believed they would judge him by themselves. And they who so fully knew and appreciated all that Violet was must see and believe that no man whose affections were not already engaged could be thrown into intimate association with her day after day, as he had been for so many weeks, and not learn to love her for herself alone.

Then he had learned incidentally from Dr. Conly that the older daughter had married a poor artist with the full consent of her parents and grandfather, his lack of wealth being considered no objection to his suit.

Captain Raymond did not look upon wealth as the highest patent of nobility even in this republican country, but thought, in his manly independence, that his well-established reputation as an honorable, Christian gentleman, and officer of the United States Navy, made him in rank fully peer of the Dinsmores and Travillas.

And he believed they would entirely agree with him in that.

But he was not a conceited man, and felt by no means sure that Violet herself would give a favorable hearing to his suit. Under the peculiar and trying circumstances of his sojourn at Ion, he had not been able to offer her any attention, and her uniform kindness had probably been shown only to her mother's invalid guest. And as he thought of the disparity of years between them, and how many younger, and perhaps in every way more attractive men, must have crossed her path, his hopes sank very low.

Yet he was not too proud to allow her opportunity to reject him. Saying to himself, "Were I certain that she is indifferent to me, I would not give her the pain of doing so — for I know her kind heart would feel it a pain — but as I am not sure of her feelings, it is only fair and just to her to let her know of mine and abide the issue." He decided that he would not go away without speaking, yet that he would first ask the consent of her natural guardians.

He therefore seized the first opportunity when alone with Mr. Dinsmore to tell of his love for Violet, and ask if he could obtain his and her mother's consent to the prosecution of his suit.

Mr. Dinsmore seemed both surprised and moved. He did not speak for a moment, then, with a heavy sigh, "Has it come to this already, that we are likely to lose our little Vi? I don't know how either her mother or I can ever do without her, ever make up our minds to resign her to anyone else!"

"I don't wonder at it, sir," the captain said with feeling. "But may I understand that you do not object to me personally?"

"No, sir, oh no! I see no objection to you more than to any other, except disparity of years, Violet being so young; but that is not so great as it was between her parents."

"Then you give me some hope?"

"If you have won her affections, yes. How is it in regard to that?"

"I have said no word to her on the subject, Mr. Dinsmore — feeling that the more honorable course was first to ask permission of her mother and yourself — and am by no means certain that she cares for me at all except as a friend of the family and of her cousin, Lieutenant Keith. Have I your consent, sir?"

"I will talk with my daughter, captain, and let you know the result."

He rose as if to leave the room, but the captain detained him.

"Let me tell you," he said, coloring in spite of himself, "that I am not rich, having very little besides my pay."

"That is a matter of small importance," Mr. Dinsmore said in a kindly tone, "seeing that riches are so apt to take wings and fly away, and that the Master said, 'A man's life consisteth not in the abundance of the things which he possesseth.' If her mother's wealth remains, Violet will be well provided for, as I presume you are aware, yet I cannot for a moment suppose you capable of seeking her on that account. In fact," he concluded with a smile, "the child has nothing at all of her own, and her mother can, should she choose, leave her penniless."

"And I should be more than willing to take her so, if I could get her," the captain answered, returning the smile. "It would be a dear delight to me to provide her with all the things desirable by my own exertions."

"Excuse the question, Captain Raymond, but have you taken into consideration the fact that Violet's extreme youth must render her unfit for the cares and responsibilities of the motherhood of your children?"

"Mr. Dinsmore, there is not a woman in a thousand of those twice her age whom I would as willingly trust. But she shall have no care or labor that I can save her from, always supposing I can be so happy as to win her for my own."

The family had retired for the night to their own apartments. Mrs. Travilla, almost ready to seek her couch, sat alone in her dressing room in front of the brightly blazing wood fire. Her open Bible was in her hand, a lamp burning on a little table by the side of her easy chair.

Her dressing gown of soft white cashmere became her

well, and her unbound hair lying in rich masses on her shoulders lent a very youthful look to face and figure.

Her father thought, as he came softly in and stood by her side, gazing down upon her, that he had seldom seen her more rarely beautiful.

She lifted her eyes to his with the old sweet smile of filial love and reverence, shut her book and laid it on the table.

He laid his hand gently on her head, bent down and kissed her on brow, cheek and lip.

"Dear papa, won't you sit down?" she said, rising to draw up a chair for him.

"Yes," he answered, "I want a little talk with you. How wonderfully young you look tonight — so like my little girl of other days, that I feel a strong inclination to invite you to your old seat upon my knee. Will you take it?" sitting down and drawing her gently toward him.

She yielded to his wish, saying, as she put her arm about his neck and gazed lovingly into his eyes, "I am still child enough to enjoy it greatly, if I am not so heavy as to weary you, my dear father."

"I do not feel your weight unpleasantly," he returned. "You must remember I am a very strong man, and you but a slight and delicate woman. Not so plump as I could wish you," he added, pushing up the sleeve of her gown and clasping his fingers round the white arm.

"Isn't there plenty of flesh there to hide the bones?" she asked laughingly.

"The bones are well hidden, but the flesh is not so solid as I would have it."

"Ah, papa, you must not be so hard to please!" she said, with playful look and tone. "I think I'm in very good condition, am glad I'm not too heavy to sit here and play at being your own little girl again. What happy days those were! When I had not a care or anxiety except to please my earthly and my heavenly father."

"Would you like to go back to them?"

"No, dear father, your love and tender care made me a very happy child, but I have no desire to retrace my steps. I should far rather press forward to the heavenly home whither you are travelling with me — 'the rest that remaineth to the people of God,' rest from sin as well as from sorrow, pain, and care."

"'Casting all your care upon Him, for He careth for you.' He who ever liveth, He who hath all power in heaven and earth, He who has said, 'I have loved thee with an everlasting love,' 'I will never leave thee nor forsake thee.' Dear daughter, if cares and anxieties oppress you, ask yourself what right a Christian has to be troubled with them."

"None, papa," she answered humbly. "I am thankful that I can say a belief in His love and power prevents them from pressing very heavily, yet it is my grief and shame that my faith is often too weak to lift the burden entirely."

"What is the particular burden tonight?" he asked tenderly.

"My absent darlings, papa. My Elsie, now beginning with the cares of married life, my eldest son exposed to I know not what dangers and temptations."

"But with the very same Almighty Friend their mother has to watch over and protect, to comfort and sustain them."

"When such thoughts will arise, dear child, turn them into petitions on their behalf, and believing in God's willingness to hear and answer prayer, your heart may grow light. But this is not exactly what I came to talk about." Then he repeated the substance of his conversation with Captain Raymond, and asked what answer she would give.

Her surprise was as great as her father's had been, and a look of sore pain came into her face as she exclaimed, "Violet, my little Vi! Must I lose her too?"

"Perhaps not, dearest; it may be that she cares nothing for him. But you need decide nothing tonight, and must try not to let the question keep you awake."

For a moment she seemed lost in thought, then lifting to his, eyes brimful of tears, "Papa," she said tremulously, "I cannot stand in the way of my child's happiness;

therefore, I must let him speak, and learn from her own lips whether she cares for him or not."

"Yes, I think you are right. And now, daughter dear, I must bid you goodnight. But first, I want you to promise me that you will determinedly cast your cares on the Lord, and not let it rob you of needed sleep."

They had both risen, and as he spoke he took her in his arms and held her close to his heart.

"I will, papa, in obedience to Him and to you," she said, while for a moment her arm was about his neck, her head laid upon his chest.

CHAPTER XIII

On you most loves, with anxious fear I wait,
And from your judgment must expect my fate.

—ADDISON

NATURALLY ELSIE'S FIRST waking thoughts on the following morning were of Violet and her future. She was not a "match-making mamma," not at all desirous to be rid of her daughters, and had never once thought of Captain Raymond as a possible suitor for Violet.

He was not a very young man. It was difficult to realize that Vi was grown up enough for her hand to be sought in marriage be even one near her own age, much less by the father of a family whose eldest child could not be very many years younger than she.

"She surely cannot fancy him!" the mother said to herself with a sigh of relief. But instantly came the remembrance that the disparity of years had been still greater between herself and the husband she had loved with all the strength of her nature — so loved that never for a moment could she admit the idea of the possibility that any other could fill his place in her heart. What more could she ask for her beloved child, for this life, than such wedded bliss as she herself had known?

But how could she spare her, especially so soon after resigning her sweet namesake daughter to another? It was only the unselfishness of her mother love that could at all reconcile her to the thought.

She longed to know whether she were likely to be called upon to make the sacrifice, but generously resolved to use no means to discover the state of her child's feelings until the captain had spoken. In the meanwhile she would neither make an opportunity for him nor throw any obstacles in his way.

Her dressing was scarcely complete, and she had just dismissed her maid, when a tap on her dressing room door was followed by her father's entrance.

"Ah, papa! Good morning!" she said, her face growing bright with pleasure. "Are you well, my dear father?" she asked, going to him and putting her arms about his neck.

"Perfectly, my darling," he said, caressing her. "How are you? How did you sleep?"

"I am able to answer, 'Very well indeed,' to both questions, papa," she returned brightly.

"You didn't let worrying thoughts keep you awake?"

"Oh, no, sir!"

"And is your answer to Captain Raymond still the same?"

"Yes, papa," she said with an involuntary sigh.

"I don't believe you wish him success," he remarked with a slight smile and a keen, searching look into her face.

"No," she said, the tears starting to her eyes, "I had thought to keep my sweet child for years to come."

"But you have no objection to him, more than you would have to anyone else?"

"No, papa, I have learned to think very highly of him, and believe my daughter's happiness will be safe in his hands — if she loves him. Yet I trust far more in your judgment than in my own. You approve of him, do you not?"

"Entirely; yet, like yourself, am so loath to part with Violet that I shall heartily rejoice if she declares herself indifferent to him."

"I long to end my suspense in regard to that," Elsie said, "but have decided to endure it until the captain has spoken because it seems better and kinder not to embarrass her by any hint of the state of his feelings."

Her father expressed approval of her resolve. Then, as her children came trooping in for their loved morning half hour with "mamma" with the bright faces and cheery greetings to her and grandpa, he left her and went down to the parlor. There he found Captain

Raymond and rejoiced his heart with the favorable response to his request.

There was something so peculiar in the mother's gaze into Violet's face as they exchanged their morning greetings, it was so unusually keen and searching — half sad and anxious, too — that the young girl asked in surprise, "What is it, mamma?"

"My darling, you are very sweet, very precious to your mother's heart!" Elsie said with an earnest, tender kiss; then, she turned quickly away to hide the telltale moisture in her eyes.

Captain Raymond was not long in finding or making his opportunity.

It was the day before Christmas and Rosie and Walter made frequent allusion to the exchange of gifts in which they expected to share that evening. They were chatting with the captain about it in the parlor soon after breakfast. They were talking of his children also — asking if he thought they had received his presents by this time, and if they would have a tree.

Violet was sitting near, helping Rose to dress some dolls for the little cousins at the Laurels. Presently, one being quite ready, Rosie must run and show it to mamma, and Walter went with her.

The door had scarcely closed on them, leaving Violet and the captain sole occupants of the room, when he rose from his chair and, moving with some care and difficulty, took another close at her side.

"Are you not disobeying orders, sir, and in some danger of suffering for it?" she asked, looking at him with a mischievous smile.

"No, I have the doctor's permission to try the ankle a little today," he answered. Then, with a slightly embarrassed air, "Miss Travilla," he said, "I should like to — would you accept a Christmas gift from me?"

"You are very kind, sir," she said, blushing vividly, "but I think I must decline. Mamma highly disapproves of young girls accepting presents from their gentlemen friends."

"But I have consulted her and your grandfather in

regard to this, and obtained their permission to offer it and ask for a return in kind. Will you accept my hand (the heart you have already won) and give me yours in exchange? Ah, I fear that you must think my presumption great! I know I am asking what a king might covet. I know that you, in your peerless beauty — so fair, so sweet, so good, so talented, so admired and sought after — are worthy of a throne. And I have not even wealth to offer you — nothing, in fact, but the love of a man whose honor is sustained, and who would cherish you as the apple of his eye. Ah, dearest girl, I have no words to express the strength and power of the passionate affection with which you have inspired me!"

All this and much more in the same strain was poured out so rapidly and ardently that Violet seemed overwhelmed by the torrent of words that had come rushing upon her so unexpectedly and without any warning.

A deep blush overspread the fair face and neck, while her work fell from her hand and her eyes sought the floor.

When at length he paused for a reply, she started up, saying confusedly and in low, tremulous tones, "I — I am far from meriting the praises you have heaped upon me, and I am very young and foolish — not fit for — for so noble and good a man — so worthy to be highly honored. And I — oh, how could I leave my dear, widowed mother!" Then, as approaching footsteps were heard in the hall without, she turned and fled from the room.

"Ah, grandpa's little Cricket, what is it? What has disturbed you so?" asked a well-known voice, in tones that spoke more pleasure than alarm. Vi, as she hurried through the hall, half blinded by the tears in her eyes, felt herself closely clasped by two strong arms that held her fast.

"Oh, grandpa! I — I wish he hadn't!" she stammered, dropping her face on his shoulder and bursting into tears.

"Who, my pet? Who has dared to ill use you?" he asked, caressing her.

Vi lifted her head and looked up at him in surprise, for certainly his tone was more amused than angry or stern. Then at a sudden remembrance of the captain's assertion that he had sought and obtained her grandfather's permission to offer her his hand, she said, "Oh, grandpa, why did you let him?" And again hiding her blushing face, "You know I could never, never leave mamma!"

"I am glad to hear it!" he returned with satisfaction, repeating his caresses, "for I don't know what either she or I could do without you. And that was your answer to Captain Raymond?"

"Yes, sir,"

"Very well, go and tell your mamma about it — she will be glad as I am to hear that we are not to lose our darling little Vi — while I see what I can say to comfort the captain."

He released her as he spoke and she flew to do his bidding.

Rosie and Walter were still with their mother in her dressing room, but as Violet came in with her flushed, agitated face, they were gently bidden to run away for a little while.

As the door closed on them, Violet dropped on her knees by her mother's chair and laid her head in her lap, hiding her face.

"My dear child! My dear, precious little daughter!" Elsie said, softly smoothing the golden tresses.

"Mamma, you know?"

"Yes, dearest."

"Oh, mamma, I can't leave you! How could I?"

"Dear child! It would be a sore trial to have to part with you, and I cannot be sorry that you are not ready or willing to go. You are one of the very great blessings and comforts of your mother's life!"

"Dearest mother, thank you! They are very sweet words to hear from your lips," Violet said, lifting her face to look up into her mother's with a beautiful smile.

"And so you have said your suitor nay?" Elsie asked with playful look and tone.

"I hardly know what I said, mamma, except that I was too young and foolish and couldn't leave you!"

"You do not care for him at all?"

"I — I don't know, mamma!" and the sweet, innocent

face was suffused with blushes. "I had never thought of his fancying me — hardly more than a child — while he — mamma, is he not very noble and good and wise? And so brave and unselfish! You know how he risked his life to save a poor old Negress, and how much he has suffered in consequence, and how patiently he has borne it all!"

"And how handsome he is?"

"Yes, mamma, one reads nobility of his nature in his face, and his bearing is soldierly."

"Ah, my little girl! My heart misgives me that I hold you by a very frail tenure!" Elsie sighed between a smile and a tear, as she bent her head to look searchingly into the depths of the azure eyes.

Violet's face crimsoned, and her head went down again into her mother's lap.

"Mamma, you need not fear," she said, very low and tremulously, "I have rejected his offer, and I cannot leave you."

"I am much mistaken if he is so easily repulse," Elsie said. "He is a brave soldier, and will renew the assault or raise the siege of my daughter's heart until he has brought it to a full if not unconditional surrender."

"Mamma, I wish I could run away."

"Come, then, to the Laurels with me, and you need not return until bedtime tonight, unless you choose."

Vi's face brightened, then clouded again. "Thank you, mamma, I will go. Yet, it will be putting off the evil day for but a very little while."

"It will give you time to think and analyze your own feelings, so that you will be better prepared for the next assault," was the playful rejoinder. "Go now, dear child, and make yourself ready. The carriage will be at the door almost immediately — Arthur has consented to my taking the children in a closed carriage. They must return before sundown, but you need not be in such haste."

Mr. Dinsmore did not find Captain Raymond looking so completely cast down as he had expected. His face was slightly flushed, his expression somewhat perplexed and disappointed, but by no means despairing.

"I fear I have been too hasty," he said in answer to his host's inquiring look. " 'The more haste the less speed,' as the old proverb has it. I fear I frightened the dear girl by too sudden and vehement an avowal of my passion. Yet I trust it may not be too late to retrieve my error."

"She rejected your suit?" Mr. Dinsmore said interrogatively.

"Yes, she seemed to do so!" sighed the lover, "yet the objections she urged are not insurmountable. She calls herself too young and foolish, but I hope to convince her that is a mistake. Young she is indeed, but very far from foolish. She cannot leave her mother is another objection, but that I should not ask her to do — as a landlubber might," he added sportively, "would in all probability. As much of my life must be spent at sea, it would not be worth while to set up a home of my own on land, if I had a wife who preferred to live with her mother."

"Well, sir, that is certainly much in your favor," said Mr. Dinsmore. "Our greatest, almost our only objection to your is the thought of parting with the child of our love."

When Violet came home that evening, she did not join the family in the parlor, but went directly to her own apartment.

"Where is mamma?" she inquired of her maid as she threw off her hat and cloak.

"In de parlor, Miss Wi'let."

"Are the children in bed and asleep?"

"Yes, miss."

Violet opened a bureau drawer and took out several small packages. Undoing one, she brought to light the miniature of her father that she had painted. She carried it to the lamp and stood for some minutes gazing down upon the beloved face with fast-falling tears.

"Oh, papa, papa!" she murmured, "how hard it is to live without you!"

At length, closing the case and restoring it to the box whence she had taken it, she gathered up the other parcels and went first to her mother's dressing room, where she laid the little box on the dressing table. Then, she went on to the rooms occupied by her younger sister and brothers, leaving a gift for each.

Going back to her own room, she spied a letter directed to her that she had not noticed before. She had seen Captain Raymond's handwriting frequently during the weeks he had been at Ion and recognized it at a glance. The color rushed over her face and neck, and her heart beat fast.

"Agnes," she said to her maid, "you may go now. I shall not need you any more tonight," and the girl went out, leaving her alone.

Even then, she did not at once open her letter, but moved slowly back and forth for some minutes with it in her hand. Then, kneeling down she asked earnestly for heavenly guidance in this important crisis of her life.

Looking into her own heart that day, she had learned that she was far from indifferent to him who had asked her to exchange with him vows of mutual love and trust, and to be the partner of his joys and sorrows. She was not indifferent, but did she love him well enough to leave, for his sake, the dear home of her childhood and the sweet mother to whom her heart had ever clung with the most ardent affection?

CHAPTER XIV

Nor less was she in heart affected,
But that she masked it with modesty,
For fear she should of lightness be detected.

—SPENSER'S FAIRY QUEEN

VIOLET HAD LINGERED at the Laurels with her Aunt Rose for some hours after her mother returned to Ion with the children. In the meanwhile, there had been a long talk between Mrs. Travilla and Captain Raymond, in which he had pleaded his cause with all the eloquence an ardent passion could inspire.

Elsie's answer was, "If you have won my daughter's heart, her hand shall not be refused you. But she is yet too young for the grave responsibilities of married life. Nor can I reconcile myself to the thought of parting with her so soon. Therefore, I should greatly prefer to have the matter dropped, at least for the present."

The captain repeated what he had said to Mr. Dinsmore in regard to his willingness to leave Violet with her mother if only he might have her for his wife.

"That would be very pleasant," Elsie said, her eyes shining. "And so far you have the decided advantage of a suitor who would carry her away from us; but, Captain, you are a father, and the woman whom you marry should be not only a wife to you, but also a mother to your children. For that care and responsibility my little Vi is, I fear, far too young. Indeed, my mother heart can ill brook the thought of her being so burdened in the very morning of her life."

"Nor should I be willing to burden her, my dear Mrs. Travilla," he said with feeling. "She should never bear the lightest burden that I could save her from. But, my dear madam, would my children be any better off if I should remain single? I think not, and I also think that should I marry another while my heart is your daughter's, I should be doing very wrong. But I cannot. If I fail to win her, I shall remain as I am to the end of my days."

"I trust not," she said, "you may get over this and meet with someone else with whom you can be very happy."

He shook his head decidedly. "I feel that that is impossible. But how was it in your own case, Mrs. Travilla? Mrs. Dinsmore is, I understand, but a few years older than yourself."

"That is quite true, sir; and I know papa never let her take any responsibility in regard to me. He taught, trained and cared for me in all respects himself. He was father and mother both to me," she said with a lovely smile, "but you, my dear sir, are so situated that you could not follow his example. You can neither stay at home with your children nor take them to sea with you."

"True, but they can stay where they are quite as well if I married as if I remain without a wife. I love them dearly, Mrs. Travilla, and earnestly desire to do my whole duty to them, but I do not think it a part of that either to do without the dear little wife I covet, or to burden her with cares unsuited to her tender years. Are you not willing to let me settle this question of duty for myself?"

"I certainly have not the shadow of a right or inclination to attempt to settle any question of duty for you, sir," she answered with sweet gentleness, "but I must, I think, try to help my dear child to consider such questions for herself. And with her, after all, must the decision of this matter remain."

Both mother and lover waited with anxiety for that decision, and while waiting the captain wrote his letter. The mother busied herself with her accustomed care and duties as daughter, mother, mistress and hostess. Each heart was lifting silent petitions that the result might be for God's glory and the best interest of all concerned.

Elsie was not surprised that Violet did not join the family that evening on her return from the Laurels.

"She doubtless wants a talk with her mother first," was her silent comment on learning that Vi had gone directly to that part of the house in which the private apartments of the family were situated. Presently, as all separated for the night, she sought her own dressing room, expecting to find Violet waiting for her there.

But the room was unoccupied. One swift glance revealed that fact, and also showed her the box Violet had left on her dressing table. Beside it were some little tokens of love and remembrance from each of the other members of the family.

A label on each told who was the giver, and breathed of tender affection to her for whom it was prepared.

She looked them over with glistening eyes, a heart full of gratitude for the loves still left her, though sore with the thought, recalled by every anniversary, of him who was gone. A sweet and beautiful smile played about her lips.

Violet's gift was the last to be taken up and examined. So life-like was the pictured face suddenly exposed to Elsie's view that it startled her almost as if he had come in and stood by her side. The label told her it was from Violet, but even without that she would have recognized it as her work; and that it was so made it all the more precious to the widowed mother.

She was gazing intently upon it, her lips quivering, the big tears dropping fast down her cheeks, as Violet, with Captain Raymond's letter in her hand, opened the door, came softly in, and glided noiselessly to her side.

"Dearest mamma," she murmured, stealing an arm about her mother's waist, "does it please you?"

"Nothing could be more like him! My darling, thank you a thousand times!"

"I painted almost entirely from memory, mamma, and it was emphatically a labor of love — love to you and to him. Oh, how sadly sweet it was to see the dear face growing day by day under my hand!"

"Has grandpa seen it?"

"Yes, mamma, he used to come in sometimes and watch me at my work. He thinks as you do of the likeness. Ah, I hear his step!" and she hastened to open the door for him.

"I thought I should find you here," he said, kissing her on both cheeks, then drawing her near the light and gazing with keen, loving scrutiny into the blushing face. "Elsie, Daughter," turning to her — "Ah!" as he perceived her emotion and took note of the miniature in her hand, "is it not a speaking likeness?"

"Yes, papa," she said in a trembling voice, going to him to lay her head on his shoulder while he clasped her in his arms, "but it roused such an intense longing in my heart! 'Oh, for the touch of a vanished hand, And the sound of a voice that is still!' "

"Dearest child!" he said tenderly, "the separation is only for time, and a long eternity of reunion will follow. 'Our light affliction, which is but for a moment, worketh for us a far more exceeding and eternal weight of glory.' "

" 'But for a moment!" she repeated. "Yes, it will seem like that when it is past, though now the road looks so long and lonely."

"Ah, dearest!" he said, softly smoothing her hair, "remember that nearer, dearer Friend whose promise is 'I will never leave thee, nor forsake thee.' "

Presently she lifted her head, wiped away her tears, and as her father released her from his arms, turned to her daughter with a tenderly interested and inquiring look.

"What is it, my darling?" she asked, glancing at the letter in the young girl's hand.

Violet gave it to her, saying, with downcast eyes and blushing cheeks, "I found it on my dressing table, mamma. It is from him — Captain Raymond — and I have written a note in reply."

"Shall I go away, Vi, and leave you and your mamma to your confidences?" Mr. Dinsmore asked playfully, putting an arm about each and looking with smiling eyes from one to the other.

"No, grandpa, please stay; you know I have no secrets from you," Violet answered, half hiding her face on his shoulder.

"And are grandpa and I to read both epistles — yours and his?" asked her mother.

"If you please, mamma. But mine is not to be given unless you both approve."

The captain's was a straightforward, manly letter, renewing his offer with a hearty avowal of strong and deathless love, and replying to her objections as he had already in talking with her mother and her grandfather.

Violet's answer did not contain any denial of a return of his affection. She simply thanked him for the honor done her, but said she did not feel old enough or wise enough for the great responsibilities of married life.

"Rather non-committal, isn't it, little Cricket?" was her grandfather's playful comment. "It strikes me that you neither accept nor reject him."

"Why, grandpa," she said confusedly, "I thought it was a rejection."

Mr. Dinsmore and his daughter had seated themselves near the table on which a lamp was burning, and Violet knelt on a hassock at her mother's feet, half hiding her blushing face on her lap.

"Ah, my little girl!" Elsie said, with playful tenderness, putting one hand under Vi's chin and lifting the fair face to look into it with keen, loving scrutiny, "were I the captain, I should not despair; the citadel of my Vi's heart is half won."

The cheeks were dyed with hotter blushes at that, but no denial came from the ruby lips. "Mamma, I do not want to marry yet for years," she said, "and I think it will not be easy for anyone to win me away from you."

"But he says he will not take you away," remarked her grandpa.

"Are you on his side, grandpa?" asked Violet.

"Only if your heart is, my dear child."

"And in that case, I am on his side, too," said her

mother, "because I desire my little girl's happiness even more than her dear companionship as exclusively my own."

"Except what belongs to her grandpa and guardian," said Mr. Dinsmore, taking Vi's arm and gently drawing her to a seat upon his knee.

Vi put her arms about his neck. "The dearest, kindest grandpa and guardian that ever anybody had!" she said, giving him a kiss of ardent affection. "Well, if you, sir, and mamma are both on the captain's side, I suppose it won't do for me to reject him. But you say my note isn't a rejection, so will you please give it to him? And if he isn't satisfied to take it for no and let me alone on the subject, he may wait a year or two and see if — if he still feels toward me as he does now, and perhaps — only perhaps — if he hasn't changed his mind and asks again —."

"You may say yes?" Mr. Dinsmore asked as she broke off in confusion.

"Oh, grandpa, say what you think best! Only don't make it too easy for him," she said, with an arch smile, but blushing deeply.

"I think," said Mr. Dinsmore, "I shall give him only your note without any additions of my own, and leave him to carry on further negotiations, or not, as he sees fit."

Captain Raymond did not take Vi's answer as a decided rejection, and within twenty-four hours had won from her an acknowledgment that she was not indifferent to him, and persuaded her to promise him her hand at some far off future day. All seemed well contented with the arrangement, and the week that followed was a very delightful one to the lovers.

In the meantime, his Christmas gifts to his children had been received by them with great joy. Especially did Max and Lulu rejoice over the opportunity now afforded them to open their hearts to their father and tell him all their grievances.

He had written to both Mr. Fox and Mrs. Scrimp directing his gifts to be delivered into the children's own hands without any examination, and never to be taken from them. Also, he directed that they be allowed to spend their Christmas together.

So Max was permitted to go to Mrs. Scrimp's to spend the day with his sisters and was well pleased to do so when he learned that the lady would not be at home, having accepted an invitation to take her Christmas dinner elsewhere.

Ann, who was left at home to look after the children, gave them an excellent dinner, and Max, having found some money in his desk, came provided with candies.

They compared presents, and spent some time over the books their father had sent, then Max and Lulu decided it would be best to write now to their father, thanking him for his gifts and telling him all they had so long wanted him to know.

Lulu compressed what she had to say into a few lines — her love, thanks, longing to see papa, Gracie's feebleness, and her own belief that it was all because she did not get enough to eat. There was also an acknowledgment that she was sometimes saucy to "Aunt Beulah," and sometimes helped herself to food, but excusing it on the plea that otherwise she too would be half starved, and that poor Max was often beaten and abused by Mr. Fox for just nothing at all.

Max's letter was much longer, as he went into more detail, and was not finished for several days. When it was, he enclosed it and Lulu's which she had given into his charge, in one of the envelopes that he had found in his desk ready stamped and directed, and mailed it to his father.

These letters reached Ion on New Year's morning. The captain read them with deep concern, first to himself, then to Mrs. Travilla and Violet, as they happened to be alone together in the parlor.

The hearts of both ladies were deeply touched, and their eyes filled with tears as they listened to the story of the wrongs of the poor motherless children.

"Oh, captain, you will not leave them there where they

are so ill used?" Vi said almost imploringly. "It breaks my heart to think of their sufferings!"

"Don't let it distress you, my dear girl," he replied soothingly. "We should perhaps make some allowance for unintentional exaggeration. There are always two sides to a story, and we have but one here."

"But told in a very straightforward way," Elsie said with warmth. "Both letters seem to me to bear the stamp of truth. Depend upon it, captain, there is good ground for their complaints."

"I fear so," he said, "and am quite as anxious, my dear Mrs. Travilla, as you could wish to set my children free from such tyranny; but what can I do? In obedience to orders, I must return to my vessel tomorrow and sail at once for a distant foreign port. I cannot go to see about my darlings, and I know of no better place to put them. I shall, however, write to Mrs. Scrimp, directing her to have immediately the best medical advice for Gracie, and to follow it, feeding her as the doctor directs. Also she is always to give Lulu as much as she wants of good, plain, wholesome food. I shall also write to Fox, giving very particular directions in regard to the management of my son."

CHAPTER XV

Great minds, like heaven, are pleased in doing good.

CAPTAIN RAYMOND'S DEPARTURE left Violet more lonely than his coming had found her, much as she was at that time missing her elder sister and brother.

They were to correspond, but as he would sail immediately for a foreign port, the exchange of letters between them could not, of course, be very frequent.

Her mother, grandpa, and Grandma Rose all sympathized with her in the grief of separation from the one who had become so dear, and exerted themselves to cheer and comfort her.

She and mamma were bosom companions, and had many a confidential chat about the captain and his poor children. The desire to rescue the children from their tormentors and make them very happy was growing in the hearts of both.

As the captain had not enjoined secrecy upon them in regard to the letters of Max and Lulu, and it was so much the habit of both to speak freely to Mr. and Mrs. Dinsmore — especially the former — of all that interested themselves, it was not long before they too had heard, with deep commiseration, the story of the unkind treatment to which Max, Lulu and Gracie were subjected.

"We must find a way to be of service to them," Mr. Dinsmore said. "Perhaps by instituting inquiries among our fiends and acquaintances we may hear of some kind and capable person able and willing to take charge of them, and to whom their father would be willing to commit them."

"I wish we could!" Elsie said with a sigh. "I think I can fully sympathize with the poor things, for I have not forgotten how in my early childhood I used to long and weep for the dear mamma who had gone to heaven, and my dear papa away in Europe."

"A very poor sort of father he was then, very culpably neglectful of his little motherless child," Mr. Dinsmore said in a remorseful tone, regarding her with a tenderly affectionate look.

"But afterward and to this day, the very best of fathers," she responded, smiling up at him. "Dear papa, what a debt of gratitude do I not owe you for all the love, care, and kindness shown by you to me and my children!"

"I feel fully repaid by the love and obedience I receive in return," he said, seating himself on the sofa by Vi's side and softly stroking her hair.

"Children and grandchildren all rise up and call you blessed, dear papa," Elsie said, laying down the embroidery with which she had been busy, and coming to his other side she put her arm about his neck and gazed lovingly into his eyes.

A silent caress as he passed his arm around her waist and drew her closer to him was his only response.

"Grandpa and mamma," said Vi, "don't you think Captain Raymond is to pitied? Just think! He has neither father nor mother, brother nor sister, no near and dear ones except his children, and from them he is separated almost all the time."

"Yes," said Mr. Dinsmore, "I do indeed! But I am not sorry enough for him to give you up to him yet. I would not allow your mamma to marry till she was several years older than you are now."

"No, sir," said Elsie smiling, "I well remember that you utterly forbade me to listen to any declarations of love from man or boy, or to think of such things if I could possibly help it."

"Well, you lost nothing by waiting!"

"Lost? Oh, no, no papa!" she cried, dropping her head on his shoulder, while scalding tears fell to the memory of the husband so highly honored, so dearly loved.

"My dear child! My poor dear child!" her father said

very low and tenderly, pressing her closer to his side. "The separation is only for the little while of time, the reunion will be for the endless ages of eternity."

"A most sweet and comforting thought, dear father," she said, lifting her head and smiling through her tears. "And with that glad prospect and so many dear ones left me, I am a very happy woman still."

At that moment there was an interruption that for a long time put flight all thought of effort on behalf of Captain Raymond's children. Herbert and Harold came hurrying with the news that a summons to Roseland had come for their grandpa, grandma, and mother. Mrs. Conly had had another stroke, was senseless, speechless, and apparently dying; also, the shock of her seizure had prostrated her father, and Arthur considered him dangerously ill.

The summons was promptly obeyed, and Violet was left in temporary charge of the children, house and servants.

Mrs. Conly died that night, but the old gentleman lingered for several weeks, during which time his son was a constant attendant at his bedside — either Rose or Elsie almost always sharing the watch and labor of love.

At length all was over. The spirit had returned to God who gave it, the body had been laid to rest in the family vault. Mr. Dinsmore and his wife and daughter went home to Ion, and life there fell back into its old quiet grooves.

They spoke tenderly of the old grandfather, and kept his memory alive in their loving hearts. But he had gone to his grave like a shock of corn fully ripe, and they did not mourn his death with the sadness they might have felt had it been that of a younger member of the family.

Toward spring, Captain Raymond's letters became urgent for a speedy marriage. He expected to be ordered home in June and allowed a rest of some weeks or months. Then he might be sent to some distant quarter of the globe, and not see his native land again for a long while, perhaps years. Under such circumstances, how could he wait for his little wife? Would not she and her mother and grandfather consent to let him claim her in June?

The tender hearts of Elsie and Violet could not stand against his appeals. Mr. and Mrs. Dinsmore felt for him, too, and at length consent was given, and preparations for the marriage were set afoot.

Then the talk about the captain's children was renewed, and Vi said, with tears in her sweet azure eyes, "Mamma, I do feel like being a mother to them — especially for his sake — if only I were old enough and wise enough to command their respect and obedience. Ah, mamma, if only you could have the training of them! Yet I could not bear to have you so burdened."

"I have been thinking of it, Vi, dear," Elsie said. "Perhaps we could give them a happy home here and help them grow up to good and noble man and womanhood, if their father would delegate his authority to your grandpa and you and me. I think we would not abuse it, but without it 'twould be quite useless to undertake the charge."

"Dear mamma!" cried Vi, her eyes shining, "how good, how kind, and unselfish you always are!"

Mr. Dinsmore, entering the room at the moment, asked playfully, "What is the particular evidence of that patent at this time, Vi?"

She answered his question by repeating what her mother had just said.

"I have a voice in that," he remarked, with a grave shake of his head. "I do not think, daughter, that I can allow you to be so burdened."

She rose, went to him where he stood, and putting her arms about his neck, her eyes gazing fondly into his, said, "Dear papa, you know I will do nothing against your wishes, but I am sure you will not hinder me from doing any work the Master sends me?"

"No, dear child, you are more His than mine, and I dare not, would not interfere if He has sent you work. But the question is, has He done so?"

"If you please, papa, we will take a little time to consider that question, shall we not?"

"Yes," he said, "it need not be decided today. The

right training and educating of those children would certainly be a good work, and could it be so managed that I could do all the hard and unpleasant part of it —," he said musingly.

"Oh, no, no, my dear father!" she hastily interposed, as he paused, leaving his sentence unfinished, "the work should be mine if undertaken at all."

"Perhaps," he said, "it might be tried for a short time as a mere experiment, to be continued only if the children do not prove ungovernable, or likely to be an injury to our own — for our first duty is to them."

"Yes, indeed, papa!" responded his daughter earnestly. "And nothing can be really decided upon until Captain Raymond comes. He may have other plans for his children."

"Yes, it is quite possible he may think best to place Max and Lulu at school somewhere."

"But poor little sick Gracie!" said Violet, the tears springing to her eyes. "Mamma, I do want to have her to love and caress, and I think we had her here with our good old mammy to nurse her and Cousin Arthur to attend her, she might grow to be strong and healthy."

"Dear child! I am glad to hear you say that!" said Elsie, "for it is just as I have been thinking and feeling. My heart yearns over poor motherless children, that little feeble one very especially."

Captain Raymond was deeply touched when, shortly after his arrival at Ion to claim his bride, he learned what was in her heart and her mother's toward his children.

After due deliberation it was settled that the experiment should be tried. Arrangements were made for the whole family to spend the summer in two adjoining cottages at a lovely seaside resort on the New England coast. Mrs. Dinsmore would be mistress of one house, Violet of the other, while the captain could be with her, which he had reason to expect would be for several months.

In the fall he would probably be ordered away; then Violet would return to Ion with her mother and the rest of the family, taking his children with her if Mr. Dinsmore and Elsie should still feel willing to take them in charge. He had a high opinion of Dr. Conly's skill as a physician, and was extremely anxious to place Gracie under his care. Also, he thought that to no other person in the world would he so joyfully commit his children to be trained up and educated as to Mr. Dinsmore, his daughter and granddaughter. And he was more than willing to delegate to them his own authority during his absences from home.

The marriage would take place at Ion, the bride and groom start northward the same day on a wedding tour. On the return trip to the spot which was to be their home for the summer, they would call for the captain's children.

In the meantime, the others would take possession of their seaside cottage.

It was a sore disappointment to the whole family at Ion, but especially to Violet and her mother, that Elsie Leland could not be present at the wedding. Lester's health was almost entirely restored, but he felt it important to him as an artist to prolong his stay in Italy for at least some months.

Edward had remained with them through the winter, had left them in April intending to make an extensive European tour before returning to his native land, but would surely hasten home for Vi's wedding if his mother's summons reached him in time.

CHAPTER XVI

Here love his golden shafts employs, here lights
His constant lamp, and waves his purple wings.

ROWLY

IT WAS SATURDAY EVENING. Edward Travilla, travelling leisurely through France, had stopped in a village not many miles from Paris to spend Sunday.

Having taken his supper and afterward a stroll through the village, he retired to his room to read and answer a sack of letters just received from America.

The first he opened was from his mother. It told of Violet's approaching marriage and urged his immediate return that he might be present at the ceremony.

"We are longing to see you," she wrote, "your mother more, I believe, than anyone else. If you have not had enough of Europe yet, my dear boy, you can go back again soon, if you wish, perhaps taking some of us with you. And Vi will be sorely disappointed if you are not present on the occasion so important to her."

"I must certainly go," he mused, laying down the letter. "I should not like to miss it. Vi will be as lovely a bride as Elsie was. I have never been able to decide which of the two is more beautiful. But I wonder that she is allowed to marry so young — just nineteen! I should have had her wait a year or two at least."

There was a step in the hall without, a rap on the door. "Come in," Edward said, and Ben appeared.

"Marse Ed'ard, dey tells me dars a 'Merican gentleman bery sick in de room cross de hall hyar; gwine ter die, I reckon."

"Indeed!" Edward said with concern. "I should be glad

~ 127 ~

to be of assistance to him. Is he quite alone, Ben? I mean has he no friends with him?"

"I b'lieves dar's a lady 'long wid him, Marse Ed'ard, but I mos'ly has to guess 'bout de half ob what dese Frenchmen say."

"You don't know the name, Ben?"

"No, sah, couldn't make it out de way dey dispronounces it. But I understands, sah, dat dese folks — meanin' de sick gentleman and de lady — and we's de only 'Mericans in de town."

"Then here, Ben, take my card to the lady and ask if I can be of service to them. Say that I am a countryman of theirs and shall be most happy to do anything in my power."

Ben came back the next moment with a face full of grave concern. "Marse Ed'ard," he said, "it's Mistah Love and Miss Zoe."

"Is it possible!" cried Edward, starting up. "And he is really so very ill?"

"Berry sick, Marse Ed'ard, looks like he's dyin' sho nuff."

"Oh, dreadful! And no one with him but his daughter?"

"Dat's all, sah. De young lady come to de do', and when I give her de card, she look at it and den at me an' say, 'Oh, Ben! I thought we hadn't a friend in all dis country! And papa is so very sick! Please, tell Mr. Travilla we'll be glad to see him.'"

Edward went to them at once, bidding Ben remain near at hand lest he should be needed to do some errand.

The Loves had remained in Rome for a few weeks after Elsie's marriage, during which Edward had met them frequently, his liking for the father and admiration of the daughter's beauty and sprightliness increasing with every encounter.

He had found Mr. Love a sensible, well informed Christian gentleman. The daughter was a mere child — only fifteen — extremely pretty and engaging, but evidently too much petted and indulged, her father's spoiled darling.

Edward knew that she was an only child and

motherless, and was much shocked and grieved to hear that she was likely to lose her only remaining parent.

Zoe herself opened the door in answer to his gentle rap.

"Oh, Mr. Travilla!" she said, giving him both hands in her joy at seeing a friendly face in this hour of sore distress, but with tears streaming down her cheeks, "I am so glad you have come! Papa is so sick, and I don't know what to do, or where to turn."

"My poor child! We must hope for the best," Edward said, pressing the little hands compassionately in his. "You call upon me for help and let me do whatever I can for you and your poor father, just as if I were his son and your brother."

"Oh, thank you! You are very kind. Will you come now and speak to him?" and she led the way to the bedside.

"Travilla!" the sick man exclaimed, feebly holding out his hand. "Thank God for sending you here!"

Edward took the offered hand in his saying with an effort to steady his tones, "I am glad indeed to be here, sir, if you can make use of me, but very sorry to see you so ill."

The hand he held was cold and clammy and death had plainly set his seal upon the pale face on the pillow.

"Shall I send Ben for a physician?" Edward asked.

"Thank you. I have had one. He will be here again presently, but can do little for me," the sick man answered, speaking slowly and with frequent pauses. "Zoe, my darling, go into the next room for a moment, dear. I would be alone with Mr. Travilla for a little while."

The weeping girl obeyed at once, her father following her with eyes that were full of anguish.

" 'Leave thy fatherless children, I will preserve them alive,' "repeated Edward in low tones, tremulous with deep sympathy.

How this scene brought back that other, but a year and a half ago, when his own father lay wrestling with the king of terrors!

"Yes, yes, precious promise! For she will soon be that, my poor darling!" groaned the sufferer. "That I must leave her alone in the world, without one near relative, alone in a strange land, penniless, too, oh this is the bitterness of death!"

"I will be a friend to her, sir," Edward said with emotion, "and so I am sure will my mother and grandfather when they learn her sad story. Tell me your wishes in regard to her, and I will do my best to see them carried out."

As briefly as possible, for his strength was waning, Mr. Love made Edward acquainted with the state of his affairs. He had retired from business the previous year with a comfortable compensation, and being somewhat out of health, had taken a European tour with the hope of benefit, if not entire recovery.

The improvement had been very decided for a time, but within the last few days distressing news had reached him from America. The news was of the failure, through the extensive speculation of one of its officers, of a bank in which the bulk of his savings had been invested.

He had other property, but as the law made each stockholder liable for double the amount of his stock, that too was swallowed up and he was thus utterly ruined.

The terrible shock of disaster had so increased his malady that it had become mortal; he was too utterly prostrate to rally from it. He knew his hours on earth were numbered.

He had a little ready money with him, enough he thought to pay his funeral expenses and Zoe's passage back to her native land, but such a mere child as she was, always used to depending upon him to see to all their affairs, she would not know how to manage, and would probably be robbed of the little she had. And even if she should arrive safely in her own country, what was to become of her then? She would be without means, would have no one upon whom she had any claim for assistance, and was too young and ignorant to do anything to earn her own living.

Edward was deeply moved by the sad recital. "My dear Mr. Love," he said, "make yourself quite easy about Miss Zoe. I will attend to all these matters about which you have spoken. I am about to return home myself, and will be her companion and protector on the voyage. Nor shall she want for friends or any needed assistance after we arrive."

"God bless you! You have lifted a heavy load from my heart!" faltered the dying father, with a look of deep gratitude. "You are young, sir, but I can trust you fully. There are few older men whom I would as willingly trust."

"And you can die in peace, trusting in the Savior of sinners?"

"Yes, He is all my hope, all my trust."

"I have been told there is a Protestant minister in the village. Shall I send Ben for him?"

"Yes, thank you. I should be glad to see him, though I feel that he or any man could be of little assistance to me now, if the work of repentance and faith has been left for this hour."

Edward went to the door, called Ben and sent him on the errand, then coming back to the bedside, "Mr. Love," he said, flushing and speaking with some little hesitation, "will you give your daughter to me if she is willing?"

"Give her to you?" the sick man asked as if not fully comprehending.

"Yes, sir, give her to me to wife, and I will cherish her to life's end."

There was a flash of joy in the dying eyes, quickly succeeded by one of hesitation and doubt. "Is it love or compassion only that moves you to this most generous offer?" he asked.

"It is both," Edward said. "I have admired and felt strongly attracted to her from the first day of our acquaintance, though I did not recognize it as love until now. We are both so young that I should not have spoken yet but for the peculiar circumstances in which we are placed. But I truly, dearly love the sweet girl and earnestly desire to be given the right to protect, provide for and cherish her as my dearest earthly treasure so long as we both shall live."

"But your friends, your relatives?"

"I think my mother would not object, if she knew all. But I am of age, so have an undoubted right to act for myself even in so vitally important a matter."

"Then if my darling loves you, let me see you united before I die."

At this moment the door of the adjoining room opened and Zoe's voice was heard in imploring, tearful accents. "Mayn't I come back now? Oh, papa, I cannot stay away from you any longer!"

Edward hastened to her, and taking both her hands in his, said, "Dear Miss Zoe, I love you, I feel for you, I want to make you my very own, if you can love me in return, that I may have the right to take care of you. Will you be my dear little wife? Will you marry me now, tonight, that your father may be present and feel that he will not leave you alone and unprotected?"

She looked up at him in utter surprise, then seeing the love and pity in his face, burst into a passion of grief.

"Leave me! Papa is going to leave me?" she cried. "Oh, no, no! I cannot bear it! He must, he will get better soon! Oh, Mr. Travilla, say that he will!"

"No, my darling!" replied a quivering voice from the bed, "I shall not live to see the morning light, and if you love Mr. Travilla, tell him so and let me see you married before I die."

"Can you, do you love me, dear little Zoe?" Edward asked in tenderest tones, passing his arm about her waist.

"Yes," she said half under her breath, with a quick glance up into his face, then hid her own on his chest, sobbing. "Oh, take care of me! For I'll be all alone in the wide world when dear papa is gone."

"I will," he said, pressing her closer, softly pushing back the fair hair from the white temple and touching his lips to it again and again. "God helping me, I will be to you a tender, true, and loving husband."

"Come here, Zoe, darling," her father said, "our time grows short." Edward led her to the bedside.

"Oh, papa, papa!" she sobbed, falling on her knees and laying her wet cheek to his.

Edward, with heart and eyes full to overflowing, moved softly away to the farther side of the room, that in this last sad time the constraint of even his presence might not be felt.

Low sobs and murmured words of tenderness and fatherly counsel reached his ears, and his heart went up in silent prayer for both the dying one and her just about to be so sorely bereaved.

Presently footsteps approached the door opening into the passage. A gentle tap followed, and he admitted the minister who had been sent for, beckoning Ben to come in also.

A few whispered words passed between Edward and the minister, then both drew near the bed.

A brief talk with the dying man, in which he professed himself ready and willing to depart, trusting in the atoning blood and imputed righteousness of Christ, a short fervent prayer for him and his child, then Edward, leaning over the still kneeling Zoe, whispered "Now, dearest!"

The tear dimmed eyes looked up inquiringly.

"We are going to belong to each other, are we not?" he said very low and tenderly. "The minister is ready now to speak the words that will make us one for the rest of our lives."

Without speaking she rose, wiping away her tears, put her hand within his arm, and the ceremony began.

When it was over, Edward took her in his arms, saying softly as he pressed his lips again and again on her forehead, her cheeks, her lips, "My wife, my own dear little wife!"

"My child! My darling!" murmured the father, feebly reaching for her hand.

Edward took it and put it into his.

The dying fingers closed feebly over it. "Lord, I thank thee for this great mercy! 'Now lettest thou thy servant depart in peace.'"

The words came low and faintly from the lips already growing cold in death, a gasp for breath followed, and all was still — no sound in the room but Zoe's wild weeping, while with silent caresses Edward held her to his heart.

They laid him to rest in the nearest Protestant cemetery, for such had been his request.

In answer to a question from her young husband, Zoe said, "No, no. I shall not wear mourning! I detest it, and so did papa. He made me promise I would not wear it for him. I shall dress in white whenever it is suitable. That is if you like it," she added quickly. "Oh, I shall try to please you always, dear Edward, for you are all I have in the world, and so, so dear and good to me!" and her head went down upon his shoulder.

"My darling little wife!" he said, holding her close, "you are so dear and lovely in my eyes that I find you beautiful in everything you wear. Yet I am glad you do not care to assume that gloomy dress."

There was no time to be lost if they would catch the next steamer for America, which Edward felt it important to do, so within an hour after the funeral they were en route for Paris, and that night found them on board, beginning their homeward voyage.

Zoe, in deep grief, shrank from contact with strangers and clung to her young husband. So they kept themselves much apart from their fellow passengers. Edward devoted himself to Zoe, soothing her with fond endearing words and tender caresses, and every day their hearts were more closely knit together.

But she seemed half-afraid to meet his kindred.

"What if they dislike and despise me?" she said. "Oh, Edward, if they do, will you turn against me?"

"Never, my love, my darling! Have I not promised to love and cherish you to life's end? But if you knew my sweet mother, you would have no fear of her. She is a tender mother, and her kind heart is large enough to take you in among the rest of her children. You saw my sister Elsie in Rome — would you fear her?"

"Oh, no, she was so lovely and sweet!"

"But not more so than our mother. They are wonderfully alike, only mamma is, of course, some years older. Yet I have often heard it remarked that she looks very little older than her eldest daughter."

He talked a great deal to her of the different members of the Ion family, trying to make her acquainted with them all and their manner of life, which he described minutely.

The picture he drew of mutual love and helpfulness between parents and children, brothers and sisters, was a charming one to Zoe, who had had a lonely motherless childhood.

"Ah, what a happy life is before me, Edward!" she said, "if only they will let me be one of them! But whether they will or no, I shall have you to love me! You will always be my husband and I your own little wife!"

"Yes, darling, yes, indeed!" he answered, pressing the slight, girlish figure closer to his side.

Chapter XVII

Benedict the married man.

—Shakespeare

Violet's wedding day was drawing near and Edward had not been heard from. Still they hoped he was on his way home and would yet arrive in time. Each day they looked for a telegram saying what train would bring him to their city, but none came.

Edward had not written because a letter would travel no faster than themselves, and did not telegraph because so little could be said in that way. All things considered, it seemed as well to take his mother and the rest entirely by surprise.

He had no fear that his little wife would meet with other than kind reception, astounded as doubtless they would be to learn that he had one. But he would have the surprise come on them all at home, where no stranger eye would witness the meeting; therefore, he sent no warning of his coming lest some one of them should meet him at the depot.

Yet the first object that met his eye on turning about from assisting Zoe to alight from the train was the Ion family carriage, with Solon standing at the horses' heads.

"Ki! Marse Ed'ard, you's here sho nuff!" cried the man, grinning with satisfaction.

"Yes, Solon," Edward said, shaking hands with him. "Who came with you?"

"Nobody, sah. You wasn't spected particular, kase you didn't send no word. But Miss Elsie tole me fotch de kerridge anyhow, an' mebbe you mout be here."

"So I am, Solon, and my wife with me," presenting Zoe, who timidly held out her little gloved hand.

Solon took it respectfully, gazing at her in wide-eyed and open-mouthed wonder. "Ki! Marse Ed'ard, you don' say you's ben an' gwine an' got married? Why dere's weddin's an' weddin's in de family!"

"So it seems, Solon," laughed Edward, putting Zoe into the carriage and taking his place beside her, "but as I am older than Miss Vi, my turn should come before hers. All well at Ion?"

"Yes, sah, an' mighty busy wid de necessary preparations for Miss Wilet's weddin'."

"What an elegant, comfortable, easy rolling carriage!" remarked Zoe, leaning back against the cushions, "it's a pleasant change from the train."

"I am glad you find it so, dear," Edward responded, gazing upon her with fond, admiring eyes.

"Yes, but — oh, Edward, how will I be received?" she cried, creeping closer to him and leaning her head on his shoulder. "I can hardly help wishing I could just be alone with you always."

"Don't be afraid, dearest," he said, putting his arm round her and kissing her tenderly again and again. "When you know them all you will be very far from wishing that."

The whole family was gathered upon the veranda when the carriage drove up. As it stopped, the door was thrown open, and Edward sprang out. There was a general exclamation of surprise and delight, a simultaneous spring forward to give him an affectionate joyous greeting. Then, there was a wondering murmur and exchange of inquiring glances, as he turned to hand out a slight girlish figure, and drawing her hand within his arm, came up the veranda steps.

Elsie stood nearest of the waiting group, heart and eyes full of joyous emotion at sight of the handsome face and manly form so like his father's.

"Darling mother!" he exclaimed, throwing his free arm about her and giving her an ardent kiss. Then drawing forward the blushing, trembling Zoe. "My little wife, mother dear, you will love her now for my sake, and soon for her own. She is all ours — alone in the world but for us."

Before the last words had left his lips Zoe felt herself folded in a tender embrace, while the sweetest of voices said, "Dear child! You are alone no longer. I will be a true mother to you — my Edward's wife — and you shall be one of my dear daughters."

A gentle, loving kiss accompanied the words, and all Zoe's fear were put to flight. Glad tears rained down her cheeks as she clung about the neck of her newfound mother.

"Oh, I love you already," she sobbed.

Mrs. Dinsmore next embraced the little bride with a kind, "Welcome to Ion, my dear."

Then Mr. Dinsmore took her in his arms, saying, with a kiss and a look of keen but kindly scrutiny into the blushing face, "Edward has given us a surprise, but a very pretty and pleasant looking one. I am your grandpa, my dear."

"Oh, I am glad! I never had a grandpa before. But you hardly look old enough, sir," she said, smiling, while the blush deepened on her cheek.

The others crowded round; each had a kiss and kind word of welcome for her as well as for Edward.

Then the news of the arrival having spread through the house, the servants came flocking about them, eager to see and shake hands with "Marse Ed'ard" and his bride.

Zoe went through it all with easy grace, but Elsie noted that her cheek was paling and her figure drooping from weariness.

"She is tired, Edward. We will take her to your apartment, where she can lie down and rest," she said. "All this excitement is very trying after her long and fatiguing journey. You both should have some refreshment, too. What shall it be?"

"Thank you, mamma. I will consult her when I get her

up there, then ring and order it," Edward said, putting his arm round Zoe's waist and half carrying her up the stairs, his mother leading the way.

"There, Zoe, what think you of your husband's bachelor quarters?" he asked gaily, as he deposited her in an easy chair, took off her hat, and stood looking fondly down at her, Elsie on the other side, looking at her too with affectionate interest.

"Oh, lovely!" cried Zoe, glancing about upon her luxurious surroundings. "I am sure I shall be very happy here with you, Edward," with a fond look up into his face. Then, turning toward Elsie, she added timidly, "and this sweet mother."

"That is right, dear child," Elsie said, bending down to kiss her again, "call me mother or mamma, as Edward does, and never doubt your welcome to my heart and home. Now I shall leave you to rest, and Edward must see that all your wants are supplied."

"Oh, Edward, how sweet, how dear, and how beautiful she is!" cried Zoe, as the door closed on her mother-in-law.

"Just as I told you, love," he said, caressing her. "She takes you to her heart and home without even waiting to inquire how I came to marry in haste without her knowledge or approval."

"Or asking who I am or where I came from. But you will tell her everything as soon as you can?"

"Yes, I shall wait only long enough to see you eat something and lying down for a nap, so that you will not miss me while I have my talk with her."

Zoe, in this her first appearance among them, had produced a favorable impression upon all her new relatives. But the uppermost feeling with each, from the grandfather down, was one of profound astonishment that Edward had taken so serious a step without consulting those to whom he had hitherto yielded a respectful and loving obedience.

Elsie could not fail to be pained to find her dearly loved father and herself so treated by one of her cherished darlings, yet tried to put the feeling aside and suspend her judgment until Edward had been given an opportunity to explain.

The younger children gathered about her with eager questioning as she rejoined them on the veranda.

"I can tell you nothing yet, dears," she answered in her accustomed sweet and gentle tones, "but no doubt we shall know all about it soon. I think she is a dear little girl whom we shall all find it easy to love. We will do all we can to make her happy and at home among us, shall we not?"

"Yes, mamma, yes indeed!" they all said.

Mr. Dinsmore rose and, motioning to his wife and daughter to follow him, went to the library.

Elsie read grave displeasure in his countenance before he opened his lips.

"Dear papa, do not be angry with my boy," she said pleadingly, going to him where he stood, and putting her arms about his neck. "Shall we not wait until we have heard his story?"

"I shall try to suspend my judgment for your sake, daughter," Mr. Dinsmore answered, stroking her hair caressingly, "but I cannot help feeling that Edward seems to have strangely failed in the loving respect and obedience he should have shown to such a mother as his. He has taken very prompt advantage of his arrival at his majority."

"Yet, perhaps, with good reason, papa," she returned, still beseechingly, her eyes filling with tears.

"We will not condemn him unheard," he answered, his tone softening, "and if he has made a mistake by reason of failing to seek the advice and approval of those who so truly desire his happiness, it is he himself who must be the greatest sufferer thereby."

"Yes," she returned with a sigh, "even a mother's love is powerless to save her children from the consequences of their own follies and sins."

Edward, scarcely less desirous to make his explanation than his mother was to hear it, hastened in search of her the moment he had seen Zoe comfortably upon a sofa in his dressing room.

He found her in the library with his grandfather evidently awaiting his coming. They were seated together upon a sofa.

"Dearest mother," Edward said, dropping upon his knees by her side and clasping her in his arms, "how can I ever thank you enough for your kindness this day to me and my darling? I fear I must seem to you and grandpa an ungrateful wretch; but when you know all, you will not, I trust, blame me quite so severely."

"We are not blaming you, my dear boy, we are waiting to hear first what you have to say for yourself," Elsie answered, laying her hand fondly upon his head. "Sit here by my side while you tell it," she added, making room for him on the sofa.

He made his story brief, yet kept nothing back.

His hearers were deeply moved as he repeated what Mr. Love told him of the lonely and a forlorn condition in which he must leave his spoiled only child, and went on to describe the hasty marriage and the death scene, so immediately following. Their kind hearts yearned over the little orphaned bride, and they exonerated Edward from all blame for the part he acted in the short, sad drama.

"Cherish her tenderly, my dear boy," his mother said, with tears in her soft eyes. "You are all, everything to her, and must never let her want for love or tenderest care."

"Mother," he answered in moved tones, "I shall try to be to my little wife just the husband my father was to you."

"That is all anyone could ask for, my son," she returned, the tears coursing down her cheeks.

"Do not expect too much of her, Edward," Mr. Dinsmore said. "She is a mere child, a petted and spoiled one, I presume, from what you have told us, and if she should prove wayward and at times unreasonable, be very patient and forbearing with her."

"I trust I shall, grandpa," he answered. "I cannot expect her to be quite the woman she would have made under her mother's training; but she is young enough to profit by mamma's sweet teachings and example even yet. I find her docile and teachable, very affectionate, and desirous to be and do all I would have her."

Zoe came down for the evening simply but tastefully attired in white, looking very sweet and fair. She was evidently disposed to be on friendly terms with her new relatives, yet clung with a pretty sort of shyness to her young husband, who perceived it with delight, regarding her ever and anon with fond, admiring eyes.

It excited no jealousy in mother or sisters. Such an emotion was quite foreign to Elsie's nature and found small place in the heart of any one of her children.

Violet, in spite of the near approach of her own nuptials, was sufficiently at leisure from herself to give time and thought to this new sister, making her feel that she was so esteemed, and winning herself a large place in Zoe's heart.

Indeed all exerted themselves to make Zoe fully aware that they considered her quite one of the family. That very evening she was taken with Edward to Vi's room to look at the trousseau, told of all the arrangements for the wedding and the summer sojourn up north, and made the recipient of many handsome presents from Mr. and Mrs. Dinsmore, Elsie and Violet.

But for her recent sad bereavement, she would have been a very happy little woman indeed. As it was, she was bright and cheerful when with the family, but had occasional spell of grief when alone with Edward, in which she wept bitterly upon his chest, he soothing her with tenderest caresses and words of endearment.

Violet's wedding was strictly private, only near relatives being present. But, in accordance with the wishes of the whole family, she was richly attired in white silk, orange blossoms, and costly bridal veil.

Zoe, leaning on Edward's arm, watched her through the ceremony with admiring eyes, more than half regretting that the haste of her own marriage had precluded the possibility of so rich and becoming a bridal dress for herself — a thought which she afterward expressed to Edward in the privacy of their own apartment. "Never mind, my sweet," he said, holding her close to his heart. "I couldn't love you any better if you had given yourself to me in the grandest of wedding dresses."

"How nice of you to say that!" she exclaimed, laying her head on his chest and gazing fondly up into his face. "Didn't Captain Raymond look handsome in his uniform?"

"Yes, indeed, but don't you think I have as much reason to envy his appearance as a groom as you Vi's as a bride?"

"No, indeed!" she cried indignantly, "he's not half as nice as you are! I wouldn't exchange with her for all the world!"

"Thank you. That's a very high compliment, I think; for I greatly admire my new brother-in-law," Edward said, with a gleeful laugh, and repeating his caresses.

Chapter XVIII

My cake is dough.

—Shakespeare

It was a warm afternoon late in June.

"There! I'm done with lessons for awhile anyway, and glad of it too," exclaimed Lulu Raymond, coming into Mrs. Scrimp's sitting room and depositing her satchel of schoolbooks upon the table.

"So am I, Lu, for now you'll have time to make that new dress for my dolly, won't you?" Gracie said languidly, from the sofa where she lay.

"Yes, little pet, and ever so many other things. But oh dear! Holidays aren't much fun after all when you can't go anywhere or have any fun. I do wonder when we'll see papa again."

"Pretty soon, Lu," cried a boyish voice in tones of delight, and turning quickly she found Max at the window, wearing a brighter face than he had shown her for many a day, and holding up a bulky letter.

"Oh, Max!" she cried, "is it from papa?"

"Yes, and I'm coming in to read it to you if you and Gracie are alone."

"Yes, we are. Aunt Beulah's gone out calling and Ann's busy in the kitchen."

"Then here I am!" he said, vaulting lightly through the window.

Lulu laughed admiringly. "I'd like to try that myself," she said.

"Oh, don't, Lu!" said Gracie, "Aunt Beulah would scold you like anything."

"Let her scold! Who cares!" returned Lulu with a

scornful toss of the head, while Max, who had gone to the side of Gracie's sofa, stooped over her, and softly patting the thin pale cheek, asked how she felt today.

"'Bout the same as usual, Maxie," she said, with a languid smile.

"Oh, Max, hurry and tell us what papa says in the letter!" cried Lulu impatiently. "Is it good news?"

"First rate, girls! Couldn't be better! He's coming here next week and going to take us all away with him!"

"Oh! Oh! Oh! How delightful!" cried Lulu, clapping her hands and dancing about the room, while Gracie clasped her hands in ecstasy, saying, "Oh, I am so glad!"

"Come, Lu, sit down here beside us and be quiet," said Max, seating himself beside Gracie on the sofa, and motioning toward a low rocking chair near at hand. "I'm going to read the letter aloud, and then I have something to show you."

Lulu took possession of the rocking chair, folded her hands in her lap, and Max began.

The letter was written from Saratoga, where the captain and his bride had paused for a few days on their wedding tour, and was addressed to all three children.

He told them of his marriage, described Violet, her mother, and the life at Ion in glowing terms, spoke very highly of Mr. and Mrs. Dinsmore and the younger members of the family. Then he told of their kind offer to share their happy home with his children if they should prove themselves good and obedient.

But here Lulu interrupted the reading with a passionate outburst. "A stepmother! I won't have her! Papa had no business to go and give her to us!"

"Why, Lu!" exclaimed Max, "of course he had a right to get married if he wanted to! And I'm very glad he did, for I'm sure they must be much nicer folks to live with than Mr. Fox and Mrs. Scrimp."

"Just like a silly boy to talk so! returned Lulu, with a mixture of anger and scorn in her tones. "Step-mothers are always hateful and cross and abuse the children and won't let their father love them any more, and —."

"Now who's been telling you such lies, Sis?" interrupted Max. "There are bad ones and good ones among them, the same as among other people. And papa says his new wife is sweet and kind and good to everybody. And if she loves him, won't she want to be good to his children? I should think so, I'm sure. Now, let me read the rest of his letter."

In that the captain went on to tell of the cottages by the sea engaged for the summer, and that thither he and Violet purposed to go the next week, taking his children with them. He wound up with some words of fatherly affection and hope that brighter days than they had known for a long time were now in store for them.

There was a postscript from Violet: "I am longing to see the dear children of my husband, especially poor, little sick Gracie. I am sure we shall love each other very much for his dear sake."

"There now, Lu, you see she means to be kind to us," was Max's satisfied comment, as he refolded the missive and put it back into the envelope.

Lulu was one who never liked to retreat from a position she had once taken. "Oh, it's easy to talk," she said, "acting's another thing. I'm not going to be caught with chaff."

"See here!" said Max, showing a photograph.

"Oh, what a pretty lady!" cried Gracie, holding out an eager hand for it.

Max gave it to her, and Lulu sprang up and bent over her to get a good view of it also.

"Who is it?" she asked.

"Isn't she pretty? Isn't she perfectly beautiful and sweet-looking as she can be?" said Max, ignoring the question.

"Yes, she's just lovely; but why don't you say who she is, if you know?"

"She's papa's new wife, the new mamma you are determined to believe is going to be so hateful."

"I'm sure she won't. She does look so sweet, I just love her already!" Gracie said.

Lulu, too proud to retract, yet strongly drawn toward

the possessor of so sweet and lovely a countenance as was pictured there, kept silence, gazing intently upon the photograph which Gracie still held.

"Whose is it, Max?" asked Gracie.

"Mine, I suppose, though papa doesn't say; but we'll find out when he comes."

"Oh, I'm so glad, so glad he's coming soon! Aren't you, Maxie?"

"I never was gladder in my life!" cried Max. "And just think how nice to go and live by the sea all summer! There'll be lots of fun boating and swimming and fishing!"

"Oh, yes!" chimed in Lulu, "and papa is always so kind about taking us to places and giving us good times."

"But I can't have any!" sighed Gracie from her couch.

"Yes, papa will manage it somehow," said Max. "And the sea air and plenty to eat will soon make you ever so much stronger."

They chatted on for some time, growing more and more delighted with the prospect before them; then, Max said he must go.

He wanted to take the photograph with him, but generously yielded to Gracie's entreaties that it might be left with her till he came again.

She and Lulu were still gazing upon it and talking together of the letter — Max having gone — when Mrs. Scrimp came in, looking greatly vexed and perturbed.

She too had received a letter from Captain Raymond that day, telling of his marriage and his intentions in regard to the children. He directed also that they and their luggage should be in waiting at a hotel near the depot of the town at the hour of a certain day of the coming week when he and his bride expected to arrive by a train from the west.

There would be a two hours' delay there while they waited for the train that was to carry them to their final destination, which would allow time for an interview between the captain and herself.

The news was entirely unexpected and very unwelcome to Mrs. Scrimp. She would have much preferred to keep the little girls for the sake of the gain they were to her and for a real affection for Gracie. Also, because of having neglected to follow out the captain's directions in regard to them — Gracie in particular — she felt no small perturbation at the prospect of meeting and being questioned by him.

As was not unusual, she vented her displeasure on Lulu, scolding her because her schoolbooks and hat had not been put in their proper places, her hair and dress made neat.

"I'll put them away presently, Aunt Beulah. You'll not be bothered with me much longer," remarked the delinquent nonchalantly, her eyes still upon the photograph Gracie was holding.

"What's that?" asked Mrs. Scrimp, catching sight of it for the first time.

"Our new mamma," the children answered in a breath, Gracie's tones full of gentle joyousness, Lulu's of a sort of defiant exultation, especially as she added, "Papa's coming next week to take us away to live at home with him."

"On shipboard?"

"No, in a cottage by the sea."

"Humph! He'll soon sail away again and leave you with your stepmother, just as I told you."

"Well, I don't care, she looks kind enough and sweeter than you do."

"Indeed! I pity her, poor young thing!" sighed Mrs. Scrimp, scanning the photograph with keen curiosity. "She's very young — a mere child I should say — and to think of the trouble she'll have with you and Max!"

"We're not going to be a trouble to her," said Lulu, "we're never trouble to people that treat us decently."

"I think your father might have given me an earlier warning of these changes," grumbled Mrs. Scrimp. "I'll have to work myself sick to get you two ready in time."

"Oh, no, Aunt Beulah, you needn't," said little Gracie, "the new mamma can get somebody to make our clothes for us. Papa will pay for it."

"Of course he will," said Lulu. "You needn't do

anything but have those we have now all washed and ironed and packed up ready to go."

"That's all you know about it!" returned Mrs. Scrimp sharply. "You haven't either of you a suitable dress for travelling in, especially in company with your father's rich wife. I'll have to go right out now to the stores and buy material, get a dressmaker to come in tomorrow bright and early, and help her myself all I can. There'll be no rest for me now till you're off."

There was no rest for anybody else in the interim except Gracie. As Ann remarked rather indignantly to Lulu, "She's as cross as two sticks."

"What makes her so cross?" asked Lulu. "I should think she'd be so glad she's going to be rid of me that she'd feel uncommonly good natured."

"Not her!" laughed Ann, "she counted on the money your father pays for years to come, but he's gone and got married and her cake is dough sure enough."

"I'm glad he did," returned Lulu emphatically. "I've made up my mind that such a sweet looking lady as our new mamma must be a great deal nicer and kinder than Aunt Beulah, even if she is a step-mother."

"She is sweet-lookin', that's a fact," said Ann. "I only wish I was goin' to make the change as well as you."

The eventful day came at last to the children; all too soon to Mr. Fox and Mrs. Scrimp, neither of whom relished the task of giving account of past stewardship — for conscience accused both of unfaithfulness to the captain's trust.

The three children were gathered in the hotel parlor, impatiently awaiting the arrival of the train. Mrs. Scrimp sat a little apart, fidgety and ill at ease, though ensconced in a most comfortable, cushioned armchair. Mr. Fox paced the veranda outside, wondering if Max had dared or would dare to inform his father of the cruel treatment received at his hand, and if so, whether the captain would credit the story.

Violet and the captain had thus far had a delightful honeymoon, finding their mutual love deepening every hour, yet were not so engrossed with each other as to quite forget his children. They had talked of them frequently and were now looking forward to the coming reunion with scarcely less eagerness than the young people themselves.

"We are almost there. It's the next station," said the captain with satisfaction, beginning to collect satchels and parcels.

"Oh, I am glad!" exclaimed Violet. "I long to see the dear children and to witness their delight in being taken into — their father's arms." The concluding words were spoken tremulously and with starting tears as a gush of tender memories came over her.

Her husband understood it, and clasping her hand fondly in his, bent over with a whispered, "My darling! My own sweet precious little wife!"

She answered him with a look of love and joy. Then after a moment's silence, "Do you think, Levis, that they will be pleased that — that you have given them a stepmother?" she asked timidly and with a sigh.

"If they don't fall in love with your sweet face at first sight I shall be exceedingly surprised," he said, gazing upon her with the fondest admiration.

"Ah, I cannot hope so much as that!" she sighed. "Children are so apt to hear and treasure up unkind remarks about stepmothers. But I shall hope to win their hearts in time. It seems to me we cannot fail to love each other with such a bond of union as our common love for you."

"No, I trust not," he said, with a bright, happy smile. "I think they are warm-hearted children. I'm sure they love their father, and it does seem to me utterly impossible that they should fail to love the dearest, loveliest, sweetest little lady in the world merely because she has become that father's wife."

The whistle blew loudly, the train rushed on with redoubled speed, slackened, came to a standstill, and in another minute the captain had alighted and was handing out Violet.

"Papa! Oh, I'm so glad you're come at last!" cried a boyish voice at his side.

"Max, my dear boy!"

There was a hasty, hearty embrace, Violet standing by smiling. Then the captain said, "Violet, my love, this is my son," and Max, moved by a sudden impulse, threw his arms about her neck and kissed her in a rapture of delight, so sweet and beautiful did she appear in his eyes.

"Oh, I beg your pardon!" he stammered, releasing her and stepping back a little, afraid he had taken too great a liberty. But venturing a second glance into her face, he saw that she was smiling sweetly through her blushes.

"No apology is needed, Max," she said cheerily. "My brothers are always ready with a kiss for mamma and sisters. And since I am not old enough to be your mother, you will let me be your older sister, won't you?"

"Oh, thank you, yes!" said Max. "Papa, let me carry the parcels. My sisters are waiting for us there in the hotel on the other side of the street. Gracie couldn't run across as I did, and Lu stayed with her."

"That was quite right," said his father. "I am in great haste to see my darlings, but would rather not do so in a crowd."

There was a very strong affection between the captain and his children. The hearts of the little girls beat fast, and their eyes filled with tears of joy as they saw him cross the street and come into the room where they were. With a cry of joy they threw themselves into his arms, and he clasped both together to his heart, caressing them over and over again. Violet looked on with eyes brimful of sympathetic tears.

The next moment the captain remembered her, and releasing the children, introduced her. "This, my darlings, is the sweet lady whose picture I sent you the other day. I am sure you will love her for papa's sake and her own too."

"Will you not, dears?" Vi said, kissing them in turn. "I love you already because you are his."

"I think I shall," Lulu said emphatically, after one long,

searching look into the sweet azure eyes; then, she turned to her father again.

But Gracie, putting both arms round Violet's neck, held up her face for another kiss, saying in joyous tones, "Oh, I do love you now! My sweet, pretty new mamma!"

"You darling!" responded Violet, holding her close. "I've wanted to have you and nurse you well again ever since I heard how weak and sick you were."

The words, reaching the ear of Mrs. Scrimp as she hovered in the background, brought a scowl to her brow. "As if she — an ignorant young thing — could do better for the child than I!" she said to herself.

"Ah, Mrs. Scrimp!" the captain said, suddenly aware of her presence, and turning toward her with outstretched hand, "How d'ye do? Allow me to introduce you to Mrs. Raymond." Violet offered her hand and was given two fingers, while a pair of sharp black eyes looked coldly and fixedly into hers.

Violet dropped the fingers, seated herself, and drew Gracie into her lap.

"Am I too heavy for you to hold?" the child asked, nestling contentedly in the arms that held her.

"Heavy!" exclaimed Violet, tears starting to her eyes as they rested upon the little, thin, pale face. "You are extremely light, you poor darling! But I hope soon to see you grow fat and rosy in the sea air your papa will take you to."

The captain had just left the room in search of Mr. Fox, taking Max with him.

"You will have to be very careful not to overfeed that child, or you will have her down sick," remarked Mrs. Scrimp with harshness, addressing Violet. "She ought never to eat anything at all after three o'clock in the afternoon."

Vi's heart swelled with indignation. "No wonder she is little more than skin and bone, if that is the way she has been served!" she said, giving Mrs. Scrimp as severe a look as her sweet, gentle countenance was capable of expressing.

"She'd have been in her grave long ago if she hadn't been served so!" snapped Mrs. Scrimp. "I'm old enough to be your mother, Mrs. Raymond, and having had that child in charge for over two years — ever since her own mother died — I ought to know what's good for her and what isn't. She is naturally delicate, and to be allowed to overload her stomach would be the death of her. I can't eat after three o'clock and neither can she."

"A grown person is no rule for a child," observed Violet, gently smoothing Gracie's hair. "Children need to eat enough to supply material for growth in addition to the waste of the system. Was it by the advice of a competent physician you subjected her to such a regimen?"

"I've always had medical advice for her when it was needed," snapped Mrs. Scrimp.

The captain re-entered the room at that moment. He had made short work with Mr. Fox, paying his bill, and sending him away with his ears tingling from a well-merited rebuke for his savage treatment of a defenseless child.

It was Mrs. Scrimp's turn now. There was no evading the direct, pointed questions of the captain. She was compelled to acknowledge that she had followed out her own theories in the treatment of Gracie, instead of consulting a physician, even after he had directed her to seek medical advice and treat the child in careful accordance with it.

"Well, madam," he remarked with much sternness and indignation, "if my little girl is an invalid for life, I shall always feel that you are responsible for it."

"I've been mother to your children, Captain Raymond," she exclaimed, growing white with anger, "and this is your gratitude!"

"A mother!" he said, glancing from her to Vi. "I hope there are few such mothers in the world. My poor baby starved! Papa's heart aches to think of what you have had to endure," he added in moved tones, the big tears shining in his eyes, as he lifted Gracie on his knees and cuddled her tenderly.

Mrs. Scrimp rose and took an abrupt and indignant leave, her bill having already been settled.

CHAPTER XIX

NEW RELATIONSHIPS AND NEW TITLES

"ARE YOU HUNGRY, Gracie darling?" her father asked with tender solicitude.

"No, papa," she said, "we had our breakfast just a little while before Aunt Beulah brought us here."

"Well, if ever you suffer from hunger again, it shall not be your father's fault," he returned with emotion.

Taking out his watch he said, "We have a full half hour yet. Max, my son, do you know of any place near at hand where oranges, bananas, cakes and candies are to be had?"

"Oh, yes, papa! Just at the next corner."

"Then go and lay in a store for our journey," he directed, handing him some money.

"May I go too, papa?" asked Lulu, as Max set off with alacrity.

"No, stay here; I want you by my side," he said, smiling affectionately upon her.

"I'm glad you do! Oh, papa, I have wanted you so badly!" she exclaimed, leaning her cheek against his arm and looking lovingly into his face, "and so have Max and Gracie. Haven't we, Gracie?"

"Yes, indeed!" sighed the little one. "Oh, papa, I wish you didn't ever have to go away and leave us!"

"I hope to stay with you longer than usual this time, and when I must go away again to leave you in a very happy home where no one will wish to ill-use you," he said, with a glad look and smile directed toward his bride.

"No one at Ion or in any house of my dear mother's will ever show them anything but kindness and love if they are good and obedient," said Vi. "We all obey grandpa, but we love to do it, because he is so dear and never at all unreasonable."

"No, I am sure he is not," assented the captain. "And I shall esteem it a great favor if he will count my darlings among his grandchildren. How would my little Gracie like to have a dear kind grandpa and grandma?" he asked, smoothing back the curls from the little pale face.

"Oh, ever so much, papa!" she responded with a bright and joyous smile. "I never had any, papa, did I?"

"Not since you were old enough to remember."

Max did his errand promptly and well, returning just in time to go with the others on board the train.

They took a parlor car and traveled with great comfort, a happy family party — father and children rejoicing in being together again after a long separation. Violet sympathized in their joy and found herself neither forgotten nor neglected by any one of the little group of which she formed a part.

Ever and anon her husband's eyes were turned upon her with a look of such proud delight, such ardent affection as thrilled her heart with love, joy, and gratitude to the Giver of all good.

Max's eyes too were full of enthusiastic admiration whenever his glance met hers, and with boyish gallantry he watched for opportunity to wait upon her.

Gracie regarded her with loving looks and called her mamma, as if the word was very sweet to say.

Lulu alone was shy and reserved, never addressing Violet directly and answering in monosyllables when spoken to by her, yet showing nothing like aversion in look or manner.

All went well for some hours, Max and Lulu partaking freely of the fruit and confections their father had provided, Gracie much more sparingly, eating less than he would have allowed her, being a sensible little girl and fearful of such unusual indulgence.

But so unaccustomed were her digestive powers to anything but the most restricted diet, that they gave way under the unusual strain, and she became so ill that Violet and the captain were filled with alarm.

Fortunately they were rapidly nearing their destination, and were soon able to lay her upon the pretty, comfortable bed prepared for her and Lulu in the new home by the sea. The physician was summoned.

The Dinsmores and Travillas had arrived some days before and made all the arrangements for a delightful welcome to the bride and groom. Both cottages were in perfect order, and a bountiful feast, comprising all the delicacies of the season, was set out in the dining room of the cottage over which Mr. and Mrs. Dinsmore presided.

But Gracie's illness interfered somewhat with the carrying out of their plans, dividing their emotions between pity and concern for the little sufferer, and joy over the return of the newly married pair.

The feast waited while the ladies, the captain, Mr. Dinsmore and the physician were occupied with the sick child.

Max and Lulu, quite forgotten for the moment by their father and Violet, and much troubled about their little sister, would have felt very forlorn, had not Harold, Herbert, and Rosie set themselves, with the true politeness to which they had been trained, to making the little strangers comfortable and at home.

They seated them on the veranda, where they could enjoy the breeze and a view of the sea, and talked to them entertainingly of the various pleasures — bathing, boating, and fishing — in store for them.

Presently, Mr. Dinsmore came out with a prescription that he asked Harold to take to the nearest drug store.

"May I go too, sir?" asked Max. "Wouldn't it be well for me to learn the way there, so that I can do the errand next time?"

"That is well thought out, my boy," Mr. Dinsmore said, with a pleased look. "But are you not too tired tonight for such a walk? It is fully a quarter of a mile."

"No, sir, thank you; a run will do me good after being so long cramped up on the train."

"Ah," Mr. Dinsmore said, taking Max's hand and shaking it cordially, "I think I shall find you a boy after my own heart — active, independent, and ready to make yourself useful. Shall I number you among my grandchildren?"

"I shall be very happy to have you do so, sir," returned Max, coloring with pleasure.

"Then, henceforth, you may address me as grandpa, as these other young folks do," glancing at Rosie and her brothers. "You also, my dear, if you like," he added, catching Lulu's dark eyes fixed upon him with a half eager, half wistful look, and bending down he stroked her hair caressingly.

"Thank you, sir," she said, "I think I shall like to. But oh, tell me, please, is Gracie very sick?"

"I hope not, my dear. The doctor thinks she will be in her usual health in a day or two."

The boys were already speeding away.

The doctor had sent everyone out of the sickroom except Mrs. Dinsmore and Captain Raymond. The child clung to her long-absent father, and he would not leave her until she slept.

Elsie led the way to Violet's room, and there they held each other in a long, tender, silent embrace.

"My darling!" the mother said at length, "how I have missed you! How glad I am to have you in my arms again!"

"Ah, mamma! My own dearest mamma, it seems to me you can hardly be so glad as I am!" cried Vi, lifting her face to gaze with almost rapturous affection into that of her mother. "I do not know how I could ever bear a long separation from you!"

"You are happy?"

"Yes, mamma, very, very happy. I could never live without my husband now. Ah, I did not dream of half the goodness and lovableness I have already found in him. But ah, I am forgetting his children, Max and Lulu!" she added, hastily releasing herself from her mother's arms.

"I must see where they are and that they are made comfortable."

"Leave that to me, Vi dear," her mother said. "You should be attending to getting dressed for supper. I think the little sick one will fall fast asleep presently, when she can be left in mammy's care, while we all gather about the supper table — and we must have you and Zoe there in bridal attire."

"Zoe! I hardly saw her in my anxiety about Gracie!" exclaimed Violet. "Does she seem happy, mamma, and like one of us?"

"Yes, she is quite one of us. We all love her, and I think she is happy among us, though of course grieving sadly at times for the loss of her father. The trunks have been brought up, I see. That small one must belong to the two little girls."

"Yes, mama, and suppose we let it stand here for the present so that I can readily help Lulu find what she wishes to wear this evening."

"Yes, dear. I will go down and invite her up. Ah, here is mamma!" as Mrs. Dinsmore tapped at the half-open door, then stepped in. She embraced Violet with motherly affection. "A lost treasure recovered!" she said joyously. "Vi, dear, you have no idea how we have missed you."

After a moment's chat Rose and Elsie went down together to the veranda, where they found Lulu, making acquaintance with the other members of the family.

"This is a new granddaughter for us, my dear," Mr. Dinsmore said to his wife.

"Yes, shall I be your grandma, child?" asked Rose, giving Lulu an affectionate kiss.

"And I too?" Elsie asked, caressing her in turn.

"Two grandmas!" Lulu said, with a slightly bewildered look, "and neither of you looking old enough. How will anybody know which I mean, if I call you both so?"

"I think," said Mrs. Dinsmore, smiling, "it will have to be Grandma Rose and Grandma Elsie."

"Yes," said Mrs. Travilla, "that will do nicely. Now, my

dear little girl, shall I take you upstairs that you may change your dress before tea?"

Lulu accepted the invitation with alacrity. They found Violet beginning to change while her maid unpacked her trunk.

"Lulu, dear," she said, as the child came in, "You want to change your dress, I suppose? Have you the key to your trunk?"

"Yes, ma'am," taking it from her pocket.

"Agnes," said Vi, "leave mine for the present (you have taken out all I want for the evening) and unpack that other."

The child drew near her young stepmother with a slightly embarrassed air. "I — I don't know what to call you," she said in a half whisper.

Violet paused in what she was doing, and looking lovingly into the blushing face said, "You may call me cousin or auntie, whichever you please, dear, till you can give me a little place in your heart. Then, as I am not old enough to be your mother, you may call me Mamma Vi. What is it you wish to say to me?"

"Mayn't I go into some other room to wash and dress?"

"Certainly, dear," Violet answered. Turning inquiringly to her mother, "What room can she have, mamma?"

"There is a very pleasant little one across the hall," Elsie said. "If Lulu would like to have it for her own, it might be as well to have her trunk sent in before unpacking."

"Oh, I should like to have a room all to myself!" exclaimed Lulu. "I had at Aunt Beulah's. Gracie slept with her in the room next to mine."

"I supposed you and Gracie would prefer to be together in a room close to your papa's," Elsie said, "but there are rooms enough for you to have one entirely to yourself."

"Then she shall," Violet said, smiling indulgently upon the little girl. "Would you like my mother or me to help you choose what to wear tonight? I want you to put on your best and look as pretty as ever you can."

Lulu's face flushed with pleasure. "Yes, ma'am," she said, going to her trunk, which Agnes had now opened. "But I haven't anything half as beautiful as the dress your sister has on."

"Haven't you? Well, never mind, you shall soon have dresses and other things quite as pretty as Rosie's," Violet said, stooping over the trunk to see what was there.

The child's eyes danced with delight. "Oh, shall I? Aunt Beulah never would get me the pretty things I wanted, to look like other girls, you know, or let my dresses be trimmed with ruffles and lace like theirs. I used to think it would be dreadful to have a stepmother, but I'm sure it isn't always."

Violet smiled. "I hope we shall love each other very much, and be very happy together, Lulu," she said. "Now tell me which dress you want to wear this evening."

"This white muslin," said the little girl, lifting it and shaking out the folds. "I believe it's the best I have, but you see it has only two ruffles and not a bit of lace. And this sash she bought for me to wear with it is narrow and not at all thick and handsome."

"No, it is not fit for Captain Raymond's daughter to wear!" Vi exclaimed a little indignantly, taking the ribbon between her thumb and finger. "But I can provide you with better, and you may cut this up for your doll."

"Oh, thank you!" cried Lulu, her eyes sparkling. "Stepmothers are nice after all."

"But Lulu, dear," Elsie said, standing beside the little girl, and caressing her hair with her soft white hand, "that is not a pretty or pleasant name to my ear — especially when applied to so young and dear a lady as this daughter of mine," looking tenderly into Vi's fair face. "Try to think of her as one who dearly loves and is dearly loved by your father, and ready to love his children for his sake."

"Yes, and for their own, too," Violet added, "just as I love my darling little sister Rosie. Now, Lulu, I think you have no more time than to get changed. She will find everything needful in that room, will she, mamma?"

"Yes, water, soap, and towels. Can you do everything for yourself, my child?"

"Yes, ma'am, except fastening my dress and sash."

"Then run in here or call to me when you are ready to have that done," said Violet.

Lulu was greatly pleased with her room. It had a set of cottage furniture, many pretty ornaments, an inviting looking bed draped in white, and lace curtains at the windows — one of which gave her a fine view of the sea.

She made haste to wash and dress, thinking the while that their father's marriage had brought a most delightful change to herself, brother and sister.

"What soft, sweet voices they all have in talking," she mused. "Grandma Rose, Grandma Elsie, and Mamma Vi. I'll call her that, if she'll let me — it's a pretty name. I like it, and I believe I have given her a little place in my heart already."

Just then Agnes knocked at the door to ask if she wanted anything.

"Yes," Lulu said, admitting her, "I'm ready to put on my dress and would like you to button it for me."

"An' put dese on fo' you too, Miss?" and Agnes held up to the child's astonished and delighted eyes a set of pink coral, necklace, bracelets and pin, and a sash of broad, rich ribbon just matching in color.

"Oh," cried Lulu half breathlessly, "where did they come from?"

"Miss Wilet sent 'em," returned Agnes, beginning her work, "an' she tole me to ax you to come in dar when I'se done fixin' ob you, an' let her see if eberyting's right. Humph! 'Twon't be, kase you oughter hab ribbon for yo' hair to match wid de sash."

CHAPTER XX

GRANDMA ELSIE AND MAMMA VI

VIOLET WAS FINISHED DRESSING. She wore a white silk trimmed with a great deal of very rich lace, white flowers in her hair and at her throat, and looked very bride like and beautiful.

So Lulu thought as she came dancing in, full of joyous excitement over her own unusual adornment. Catching sight of Violet standing in front of her dressing table turning over a box of ribbons, "Oh, how beautiful you are!" she cried, "and how very kind to let me wear these," glancing down at the ornaments on her own person.

"Let you wear them, dear child! I have given them to you for your own, and am looking now for ribbon for your hair to match the sash. I had forgotten it. Ah, here is just the thing!"

You have given me these lovely, lovely bracelets and necklace! And this handsome sash, too!" cried Lulu in wide-eyed astonishment. "Oh, you are just too, too good to me! May I kiss you? And may I call you Mamma Vi now?"

"Yes, indeed, if you can give me a little place in your heart," Violet answered, taking the little girl in her arms.

"Oh, a great big place!" cried Lulu returning Vi's caresses with ardor. "Mamma Vi! It's such a very pretty name, and you are my own sweet, pretty new mamma!" A great deal nicer than if you were old enough to be my real mother."

"Ah, Lulu, it makes me very happy to hear all that!" said her father's voice behind her, and she felt his hand laid affectionately upon her head.

She turned round quickly. "Ah, papa! How nice you look, too! How is Gracie?"

"I left her sleeping comfortably a half hour ago, and have been getting changed in another room. Ah, my love!" gazing at Violet with proud, fondly admiring eyes, "how very lovely you are!"

"In my husband's partial eyes," she returned, looking up at him with a bright, sweet smile.

"In Lulu's, too, judging from what I heard her say just now," he said, turning his eyes to his daughter again. "Ah, how you have improved her appearance!"

"Yes, papa, only see these lovely things she — Mamma Vi has given me!" cried Lulu, displaying her ornaments.

"A most generous gift," he said, examining the jewelry. "These coral ornaments are costly, Lulu, and you must be careful of them. Mamma Vi! Is that the name you have chosen for yourself, my love?" he asked, again turning to his bride.

"Yes, if you approve, Levis?"

"I like it!" he returned emphatically.

"And the other ladies," remarked Lulu, "say I am to call them Grandma Rose and Grandma Elsie. And the gentleman told me and Max to call him grandpa."

"May I come in?" asked Max at the door, which stood wide open.

"Yes," his father and Violet both answered.

"Oh!" he cried, gazing at Violet in undisguised admiration, "how lovely, how splendid you look! What shall I call you? You said, you know, and of course anybody can see it, that you're not old enough to be my mother."

"No," she said, with a look of amusement and pleasure, "so you may use the name Lulu and Gracie will call me — Mamma Vi."

"Miss Wilet," said Agnes, appearing at the door, "dey says dey's waitin'suppah fo' you and de captain."

"Ah, then we must not linger here! Lulu dear, let Agnes tie this ribbon on your hair. She can do it more tastefully than I. Max, I see you are dressed for the evening."

"Yes, Mamma Vi, your brother Herbert showed me my room — a very nice one in the story over this — and had my trunk carried up. Am I all right?"

"You'll do very well," his father said laughingly, but with a gleam of fatherly pride in his eye. "Give your arm to your sister, and we will go down — if you are ready, little wife."

The last words were spoken in a fond whisper, close to Violet's ear, as he drew her hand within his arm, and were answered by a bright, sweet smile as she lifted her azure eyes to his.

The two cottages stood but a few feet apart, with no fence or wall of separation between, and were connected by a covered way; so that it was very much as if they were but one house.

The room in which the feast was spread was tastefully decorated with evergreens, flags and flowers; the table too was adorned with lovely bouquets and beautifully painted china and sparkled with silver and cut glass.

The Dinsmores, Travillas, and Raymonds gathered about it as one family — a bright, happy party. Edward was there with his Zoe, looking extremely pretty in bridal attire, each apparently as devoted as ever to the other.

Max and Lulu behaved themselves admirably, the latter feeling quite subdued by the presence of her father and so many elegantly dressed and distinguished looking people.

It was certainly a great change from Mrs. Scrimp's little dining room with its small plainly furnished table, the three to sit down to it, and Ann to wait upon them — a very pleasant change to Lulu. She enjoyed it greatly.

She and Max scarcely spoke during the meal, occupying themselves in eating and listening to the lively discourse going on around them. They were well waited upon, and both Elsie and Violet interested themselves to see that the little strangers were not neglected.

On leaving the table, all repaired to the veranda and front door yard for the enjoyment of a moonlight evening and the sea breeze.

The young Travillas and Raymonds speedily grew quite intimate and were mutually pleased; but the Raymonds, fatigued with the journey and excitement of the day, were ready to retire at an early hour.

They waited only for family worship, conducted for both households by Mr. Dinsmore, then Violet and they bade goodnight and went back to their own dwelling, leaving the captain to sit some time longer on the veranda with the other gentlemen.

"Have you everything you want in your room, Max?" Violet asked in a kindly tone, as the boy took up his bedroom candle.

"Yes, thank you, Mamma Vi," he answered cheerfully, but with a longing look at her.

"What is it, Max?" she asked with her sweet smile. "Don't be afraid to tell me if there is anything you want."

"I — I'm afraid I oughtn't to ask it," he stammered, blushing vividly. "I've no right, and — and it might be disagreeable, but — oh, I should like to kiss you goodnight!"

"You may, Max," she said, laughing, then put her arms round his neck and gave the kiss very heartily.

"Thank you," he cried in blushing delight, then hurried away, calling back, "Ah, goodnight, Lu!"

"Goodnight," she answered, looking wistfully at Violet.

"Shall I have a goodnight kiss from you too, dear?" Violet asked, offering her cheek.

Lulu accepted the invitation in an eager, joyous way, then asked, "May I see Gracie before I go to bed?"

"Yes, dear. We will go in very quietly lest we should wake her if she is asleep."

They found Gracie awake, Aunt Chloe shaking up her pillow and smoothing the covers over her.

"Oh, mamma!" she cried in her little weak voice, "how beautiful you are! And, Lulu, where did you get those pretty things?"

"Mamma Vi gave them to me," Lulu said. "Oh, Gracie dear, are you better?"

"Yes, I don't feel sick now, only weak. She's very

good to me, she and everybody," with a grateful look at Aunt Chloe.

"Yes," Violet said, "mammy is always good and kind, especially to a sick person. Now Lulu and I will kiss you goodnight and leave you to go to sleep again."

"You are nice and kind to come, both of you," Gracie said, receiving and returning their caresses.

"Mammy," Violet said as she turned to leave the room, "I'm afraid you are not able to take care of her through the night."

"Yes, I is, honey darlin'," responded the old woman with warmth. "I'll hab a quilt spread down dar on de flo', and I'll lie dar an' sleep, and ef de chile stirs I'll wake right up and gib her eberything she wants."

"Mamma Vi, don't you want to see my room?" Lulu asked as they neared its door. "I think it is ever so pretty."

"So it is," Violet said, stepping inside with her, "and I am very glad you like it. If you think of anything else you want in it, don't hesitate to ask for it. Both your papa and I wish to do all in our power to make his children happy."

"Thank you. Oh, it is so nice to have a — new mamma! Such a sweet, kind one," Lulu exclaimed with impulsive warmth, setting down her candle and throwing her arms about Violet's neck.

"Dear child!" Violet said, returning the embrace, "I am very glad you are beginning to love me. I hope we shall all love each other better every day and be happy together. You won't forget to ask God's protection before you sleep, and thank Him for His love and care? What a mercy that we met with no accident on our journey!"

"Yes, indeed! And I won't forget to say my prayers, Mamma Vi."

They exchanged an affectionate goodnight, and Violet went to her own room.

Agnes was there, waiting to assist her in disrobing, to take down her hair, and put things in place.

As the maid withdrew, her duty finished, Elsie came softly in.

"Dearest mamma!" cried Vi joyously, "I am so glad you have come! I thought you would."

"Yes, daughter, I have just seen Rosie and Walter in bed, and could not deny myself the pleasure of one of the old-time private talks with my dear Vi. Ah, you don't know how I have missed them ever since Captain Raymond carried you away from Ion!"

They were standing together with their arms about each other.

"Mamma," Violet said with an earnest, tenderly affectionate look into her mother's face, "How very beautiful you are! And how youthful in appearance! There is not a line in your face, not a silver thread in your hair, and it still has that exquisite golden tinge it has had ever since I can remember."

"Ah, dear child! We can see many beauties in those we love that are imperceptible to other eyes," Elsie returned with a quiet smile.

"But, mamma, everyone sees you to be both young and beautiful in looks. You look far too young to be addressed as grandma by Max and Lulu, or even Gracie. I wish you would not allow it, but let them call you auntie."

"It does not make me really any older, or even to feel or look so," the mother said, with a low silvery laugh of amusement at Violet's earnestness.

"But I don't like it, dear mamma."

"Then I am sorry I gave them permission. Yet, having done so, I do not like to recall it. But, daughter dear, old age will come to us all, if we live, and it is quite useless to fight against the inevitable."

"Yet we needn't hurry it on, mamma."

"No, but consider — had I and my eldest daughter married as early in life as my mother did, I might now have my own grandchildren as old as Max and Lulu. Besides," she added gaily, "how can I hope to deceive people into supposing me young when I have three married children?"

"Yes, mamma, that is true," Violet said, after a moment's thought, "and perhaps the children may be more ready to submit to the guidance and control of a grandma than of an aunt. Oh, how thankful I am that when their father is no longer here to govern them, they will not be left to my management alone!"

CHAPTER XXI

REBELLION

THE NEXT MORNING Violet began her housekeeping —
a not very arduous undertaking, as competent servants
had been brought from Ion for her establishment as well
as for that next door.

It was pleasant to her and the captain to sit down to a
well-appointed table of their own.

Max and Lulu too, coming in fresh and rosy from a
stroll along the beach, thought it extremely nice that
at last they had a home of their own with their father
and so sweet and pretty a new mamma to take the head
of the table.

The oysters and fish, just out of the ocean that
morning, and Aunt Phillis's cornbread and muffins were
very delicious to the keen young appetites, and as Gracie
was reported much better, everyone was in good spirits.

The captain and Violet had both been in to see her
and ask how she had passed the night before coming
down to the breakfast room.

Immediately after the meal the captain conducted
family worship. That over, Max and Lulu seized their
hats and were rushing out in the direction of the beach,
but their father called them back.

"Where are you going?" he asked.

"Down by the waves," said Lulu.

"To the beach, sir," said Max.

"Without a word to anyone!" he remarked a little
severely. "How do you know that you are not wanted
by your mamma or myself? We are going directly for a
drive on the beach and I had intended to take you both
along. Now I am inclined to leave you behind."

The children hung their heads, looking crestfallen and disappointed.

"Oh, Levis, please let them go!" pleaded Violet, laying her hand persuasively on her husband's arm. "I am sure they did not mean to do wrong."

"Well, my love," he answered, "I will overlook it for the first time for your sake. But, Max and Lulu, you must understand that you are under authority and are not to leave the house without first reporting yourselves to your mother or me and asking permission, stating where you desire to go and about how long you expect or wish to stay."

"Yes, sir," said Max, "but if you and Mamma Vi should both happen to be out?"

"Then you may go to Grandpa Dinsmore or Grandma Elsie."

"Yes, sir," Max answered in a pleasant tone, adding, "I'm sorry to have displeased you. Papa, and will be careful in the future to obey the order you've just given."

But Lulu remained silent, and her countenance was sullen. She had been so long in the habit of defying Mrs. Scrimp's authority that now she was disposed to resist even her father's control in small matters, and think she ought to be permitted to go and come at her own sweet will. The thought of being subjected to the sway of her new mother and her relatives seemed to the proud, passionate child almost beyond endurance.

The expression of her face did not escape her father's observation, but he thought it best to take no notice of it, hoping her angry and rebellious feelings would soon pass away and leave her again the pleasant, lovable child she had been a few moments since.

The carriage was already at the door.

"I think the air would do Gracie good," he remarked to Vi, "and the drive should not prove too fatiguing if I support her in my arms. We have room for one more than our party. Will not your mother go with us?"

"Thank you. I'll run in and ask her," Vi said, tripping away.

Elsie accepted the invitation, remarking gaily, "I have no housekeeping cares to prevent me. I'm just a daughter at home in her father's house," giving him a loving look and smile, "as I used to be in the glad, free days of my girlhood."

The captain came down with Gracie in his arms, hers about his neck, her little pale face on his shoulder. She looked thin and weak, but very happy.

Grandma Elsie and Mamma Vi greeted her with loving inquiries and tender kisses.

"Do you feel strong enough for the drive, dear?" asked Grandma Elsie.

"Yes, ma'am, with papa to hold me in his strong arms."

"Papa's dear baby girl!" murmured the captain low and tenderly, imprinting a gentle kiss on the pale forehead.

Mr. Dinsmore came over, handed the ladies and Lulu into the carriage, then held Gracie till her father was seated in it and ready to take her again.

It was a bright, fair morning with a delicious breeze from the sea and all enjoyed the drive greatly, unless perhaps Lulu, who had not yet recovered her good humor. She sat by her father's side, scarcely speaking, but no one seemed to notice.

Gracie was asleep when they returned, and her father carried her up to her room and laid her down so gently that she did not wake.

The others had paused on the veranda below. Zoe and Rosie came running over to say the swimming hour was near at hand, and to ask if they were going in.

"I am not," Elsie said.

"Nor I, said Violet, "I'm a little tired and should prefer to sit here and chat with mamma."

"I'd like to go in," said Max. "When papa comes down I'll ask if I may."

"Mamma," said Rosie, "I don't care to go in today, but may I go down on the beach and watch the bathers?"

"Yes, daughter. Take a servant with you to carry some camp chairs and to watch over Walter, if he wants to go with you."

"You'll come too, won't you?" Rosie said to Lulu. "It's good fun to watch the people in the water."

"I'll have to ask leave first," replied Lulu in a sullen tone. "Can you wait till papa comes down?"

"That is not necessary since your father has invested me with authority to give you permission," remarked Violet pleasantly. "You may go if you will keep with Rosie and the others. But, Lulu, my dear, I wish you would first go up to your room, take off those coral ornaments and put them away carefully. They do not go well with the dress you have on and are not suitable for you to wear down on the beach at this time of day."

She had noticed on first seeing the child that morning that she had them on, but said nothing about it till now.

"You said you gave them to me to keep!" cried Lulu, turning a flushed and angry face toward her young stepmother. "And if they are my own, I have a right to wear them when and where I please, and I shall do so."

"Lucilla Raymond, to whom were you speaking?" asked her father sternly, stepping into their midst from the open doorway.

The child hung her head in sullen silence, while Vi's face was full of distress; Elsie's but little less so.

"Answer me!" commanded the captain in a tone that frightened even insolent Lulu. "I overheard you speaking in an extremely impertinent manner to some one. Who was it?"

"Your new wife," muttered the angry child.

The captain was silent for a moment, trying to gain control over himself. Then he said calmly, but not less sternly than he had spoken before, "Come here."

Lulu obeyed, looking pale and frightened.

He leaned down over her, unclasped the coral ornaments from her neck and arms, and handing them to Violet, said, "My dear, I must ask you to take these back. I cannot allow her to keep or wear them."

"Oh, Levis!" began Vi in a tone of entreaty; but a look and a gentle "Hush, love!" silenced her.

"Now, Lucilla," he said, resuming his stern tone of

command, "ask your mamma's pardon for your impertinence, and tell her you will never be guilty of the like again."

"I won't!" exclaimed Lulu passionately.

At that her father, with a look of utter astonishment at her presumption, took her by the hand and led her into the house, upstairs and to her own room.

"My daughter," he said, "I must be obeyed. I could not have believed you would be so naughty and disobedient so soon after my return to you, for I thought you loved me."

He paused for a reply, and Lulu burst out with passionate vehemence, "You don't love me, papa! I knew you wouldn't when you got a new wife. I knew she'd steal all your love away from your own children!"

In that moment of fierce, ungovernable anger all Vi's sweetness was forgotten and old prejudices returned in full force.

The captain was too much shocked and astonished to speak for a moment. He had not dreamed that his child possessed so terrible a temper.

"You were never more mistaken, Lulu," he said at length in a moved tone. "I never loved my children better than I love them now. Are you not sorry for your rebellious reply to me a moment since? Will you not tell me so, and do at once what I have bidden you?"

"No! I'll never ask her pardon!"

"You will stay in your room in solitary confinement until you do, though it should be all summer," he said firmly, went out, locked the door on the outside, and put the key into his pocket.

Zoe and Rosie had hastened away the moment the captain appeared upon the scene on the veranda, and as he led Lulu into the house Violet burst into tears.

"Oh, mamma!" she sobbed, "what shall I do? I wish I had not said a word about the ornaments, but just let her wear them! I never meant to make trouble between my husband and his children! I never should have done so intentionally."

"My dear child, you have no cause to blame yourself," Elsie said soothingly.

"No, not a bit of it, Mamma Vi," cried Max, coming to her side. "I love Lu dearly, but I know she has a very bad temper, and I think it's for her own good that papa has found it out already, so that he can take means to help her conquer it. Dear me! I should never dare to say 'I won't' to him. Nor I shouldn't want to, because he's such a good father to us, and I love him dearly."

"Dear Max," Violet said, smiling through her tears as she took his hand and pressed it affectionately in hers. "I am sure he is a good, kind, loving father. His children could never doubt it if they had heard all he has said to me about them, and I trust you will never do anything to give him pain."

The captain rejoined them presently, asking the ladies with assumed cheerfulness if they intended swimming.

They answered in the negative, and turning to Max he said kindly, "My son, if you wish to do so, I will take you with me. The surf is fine this morning and I feel inclined to go in."

"Oh, thank you, papa!" cried Max, "it will be splendid to go in with you!"

The captain re-entered the house and Violet followed. He turned at the sound of her quick, light step, saw the distress in her face, the tears in her eyes, and was much moved thereby.

"My love, my darling!" he said, taking her in his arms, "do not let this thing trouble you. Ah, it pains me deeply that a child of mine should have already brought tears to those sweet eyes."

"Oh, Levis!" she sobbed, hiding her face on his shoulder, "forgive her for my sake. Don't insist on her asking my pardon. I would not have her so humiliated."

"There are few things you would ask, love, that I would not grant," he said tenderly, softly smoothing her golden hair. "But for my daughter's own sake, I must compel her obedience. What would become of her if left to the unrestrained indulgence of such a temper and spirit of insubordination as she has shown this morning?"

"I know you are right," she sighed, "but I cannot help feeling sorry for her, and oh it almost breaks my heart to think that I was the cause of the trouble."

"Ah, but in that you are mistaken, sweet wife," he said, repeating his caress. "Lulu's own evil temper was the inciting cause. I could see that she was in a sullen, rebellious mood from the time that I called her in before the drive. That I must begin already to discipline one of my children gives me a sad heart, but I must try to do my duty by her at whatever cost of pain to her or myself."

As her father turned the key in the lock, Lulu stamped with passion, and clenched her fists until the nails were buried in the flesh. "I'll never do it!" she hissed between her tightly shut teeth, "no, never! If he keeps me here till I die. I just wish I could die and make him sorry for treating me so!"

Then throwing herself on the bed, she sobbed herself to sleep.

She must have slept several hours, for she was waked by the opening of her door, and starting up found her father standing beside her with a small tray in his hand. On it were a plate of graham bread, a china bowl containing milk, and a silver spoon.

"Here is your dinner, Lucilla," he said, speaking in a quiet grave tone, as he set the tray on a little stand in a corner between the windows, "unless you are ready to obey me. In that case, I shall take you down to your mamma, and when you have begged her pardon and told me you are sorry for your rebellious words and conduct toward me, you can eat your dinner with us."

"I don't want to go downstairs, papa," she said, turning her face away from him. "I'd rather stay here. But I should think you'd feel mean to eat all sorts of good things and give me nothing but skim milk and that black bread."

"I give you that bread because it contains more nutrients than white," he said. "As to the good things the rest of us may have to eat, you shall share them as soon as you are ready to submit to my authority, but not till then."

He waited a moment for a reply, but receiving none, went out and locked the door.

When he came again at tea-time, bringing a fresh supply of the same sort of fare, he found the first still untouched.

Lulu was very hungry, and really for the last hour had quite longed to eat the bread and milk, but from sheer obstinacy would not touch it. She thought if she held out long enough in her refusal to eat, something better would be furnished her.

But now she fairly quailed before the glance of her father's eye as he set the second tray down and seating himself said, "Come here to me!"

She obeyed, looking pale and frightened.

He drew her in between his knees, put one arm around her, and taking the bowl he had just brought in the other hand, held it to her lips with the command, "Drink this! Every drop of it!"

When that was done, he commanded, "Now break this bread into that other bowl of milk, take your spoon and eat it."

Now thoroughly frightened, she did not dare disobey.

He sat and watched her till the meal was finished, she feeling that his stern eye was upon her, but never once venturing to look at him.

"Have you anything to say to me, Lucilla?" he asked as he rose to go.

"No, sir," she answered, with her eyes upon the carpet.

"My child, you are grieving me very much," he said, took up the tray and went out.

Lulu did love her father — though not nearly so well as her own self-will — and his parting words brought a gush of tears from her eyes. She was half inclined to call to him to come back, and say she would obey.

But no! Her heart rose up in fierce rebellion at the thought of asking pardon of his "new wife." "I'll never do it!" she repeated half aloud, "and when I get sick and die from being shut up here, papa will wish he hadn't tried to make me."

So she hardened her heart day after day and refused to yield.

Her fare continued the same, her father bringing it to her three times daily, now in silence, now asking if she were ready to obey.

She saw no one else but the maid who came each morning to put her room in order — except as she caught sight of one or another from the window. She liked to look at the sea and watch the vessels sailing by, but was often seized with a great longing to get down close to the waves.

After the second day, she grew very, very weary of her imprisonment and indulged in frequent fits of crying as she heard the happy voices of Max and the young Travillas at sport on the veranda, in the yards below, or knew from the sound of wheels, followed by an hour or more of quiet, that drives were being taken. She knew she was missing a great deal of enjoyment. Being of an active temperament, extremely fond of outdoor exercise, made this close confinement even more irksome to her than it would have been to many another.

She had nothing to do. She had turned over the contents of her trunk several times, had found her doll, and tried to amuse herself with it, but there was little fun in that without a playmate. She had no book but her Bible, and that she did not care to read — there was too much in it to condemn her.

"Papa," she said, when he came with her breakfast on the fourth day, "mayn't I go and run on the beach for ten minutes and then come back?"

"What did I tell you about leaving this room?" he asked.

"I know you said I shouldn't do it till I asked her pardon," she replied, bursting into a fit of passionate weeping, "but I'll never do that, and if I get sick and die you'll be sorry for keeping me shut up so."

"You must not talk to your father in that impertinent manner," he said sternly. "It is not I who keep you here, it is your own self-will. And just so long as that lasts you will remain here."

"I haven't a friend in the world," she sobbed. "My own father is cruel to me since he —."

"Hush!" he said in stern indignation. "I will have no more of that impertinence! Will you force me to try the virtue of a rod with you, Lucilla?"

She started and looked at him with frightened eyes.

"I should be very loath to do so, but advise you to be very careful how you tempt me to it any farther," he said, and he left her.

He went down with a heavy heart to the breakfast room where his wife, Max and Gracie awaited his coming.

All three greeted his entrance with loving smiles. Vi was looking very lovely, and he noticed with gratitude that Gracie's eyes were bright and her cheeks faintly tinged with pink. She was improving rapidly in the bracing sea air and winning all hearts by her pretty ways.

She ran to meet him crying, "Good morning, my dear papa!"

He took her in his arms and kissed her tenderly two or three times, longing to be able to do the same by the other one upstairs; then, put Gracie in her place at the table and took his own.

A tempting meal was spread upon it, but he felt that he could scarcely enjoy it because it must not be shared with Lulu.

Vi read it all in his face, and her heart bled for him. She had seen through all these days of conflict with his stubborn, rebellious child, that his heart was sore over it, though he had great efforts to appear as usual, and never spoke of Lulu except when it as quite necessary.

He had had to explain to Gracie why her sister was not to be seen, and to entreat Vi not to grieve over her unintentional share in occasioning the struggle, or let it hinder her enjoyment.

Elsie had made a generous settlement upon each of her married children, so Vi had abundant means of her own. She longed to spend some of her money on her husband's children, especially in pretty, tasteful dress for the two little girls. She asked his consent, deeming it not right to act without it.

He seemed pleased that she had it in her heart to care for them in that way, but said nothing could be done for Lulu at present. She might do what she would for Gracie, but the expense must be his — nor could she move him from that decision.

She had begun to carry out her plans for Gracie, delighting in making her look as pretty as possible — each day hoping that Lulu's submission would make it possible to do the same for her.

She knew this morning, by her husband's countenance and his coming in alone, that that hope had again failed, and her heart sank. But for his sake, she assumed an air of cheerfulness and chatted of other things with a sprightliness and gaiety that won him from sad thoughts in spite of himself.

Chapter XXII

Prithee, forgive me!

"Papa, can't I see Gracie?" Lulu asked when he came in with her dinner.

"Certainly, if you are ready to obey."

The child's lip quivered. "I'm so tired of that bread and milk," she said. "Can't I have something else? I'm sure you and everybody in the house have a great many good things.'

"We have, and it is a great grief to me that I cannot share them with my little Lulu. I have very little enjoyment in them because of that."

"Papa, I'm sorry I've been so naughty, so impertinent to you. I don't mean ever to be so again, and I'll be a good girl in every way after this, if you'll let me out."

"Then come with me to your mamma," he said, holding out his hand.

"I can't ask pardon of her," she said, turning away with a sob.

"You must, Lucilla," he said in a tone that made her tremble. "You need not think to conquer your father. I shall keep you here on this plain fare and in solitary confinement until you are entirely penitent and submissive."

He waited a moment, but receiving no reply, went out and locked the door.

"She is still stubborn," he said to Violet, whom he found alone in their room across the hall, sighing deeply as he spoke, "and the close confinement is telling upon her. She grows pale and thin. Oh, how my heart bleeds for her, my dear child! But I must be firm. This is an important crisis in her life, and her future character —

therefore her happiness — for time and eternity — will depend greatly upon how this struggle ends."

The next day was Sunday, and on returning home from church, he went to Lulu's room.

Little had passed between them since the talk of yesterday when he carried in her dinner. He found her now sitting in a listless attitude, and she did not look up on his entrance.

He lifted her from her chair, sat down in it himself, and took her on his knee.

"Has this holy day brought no good thoughts or feelings to my little girl?" he asked, gently smoothing her hair back from her forehead.

"You know I couldn't go to church, papa," she said, without looking at him.

"No, I know you could have gone, had you chosen to be a good, obedient child."

"Papa, how can you go on trying to make me tell a lie when you have always taught me it was such a wicked, wicked thing to do?"

"I try to make you tell a lie! What can you mean, daughter?" he asked her in great surprise.

"Yes, papa, you are trying to make me ask Mamma Vi's pardon after I have said I wouldn't."

"Ah, my child, that was a wicked promise because it was rebellious against your father's authority, which God commands you to respect. Therefore the sin was in making it, and it is your duty to break it."

Then he made her repeat the fifth and sixth commandments, and called her attention to its promise of long life and prosperity, as far as it shall be for God's glory and their own good, to all such as keep it.

"I want you to inherit that blessing, my child," he said, "and to escape the curses pronounced against those who refuse obedience to their parents."

Opening the Bible, he read to her, "The eye that mocketh at his father and despiseth to obey his mother, the ravens of the valley shall pick it out, and the young eagles shall eat it."

She gave him a frightened look, then, with a slight shudder, hid her face on his chest, but did not speak.

"Lulu," he said, again softly stroking her hair, "about nine years ago, I came home from a long voyage to find a dear little dark-eyed baby daughter, and as I took her in my arms, oh how my heart went out in love to her and gratitude to God for giving her to me! I loved her dearly then. I have loved her ever since with unabated affection, and never doubted her love to me until now."

"Papa, I do love you," she said, hastily brushing away a tear. "I've said I was sorry for being naughty to you and didn't mean to do so any more."

"And yet are continuing to be naughty and disobedient all the time. It is quite possible, Lulu that you may some day be fatherless. If that time should come, do you think you will look back with pleasure to these days of rebellion?"

At that she cried quite bitterly, but her father waited in vain for a word of reply.

He put her on her knees on the floor, knelt beside her, and with his hand on her head, prayed earnestly, tenderly that the Lord would cast out her wicked temper, forgive her sins, give her a new heart, and make her his own dear child.

Rising, he took her in his arms again for a moment, she still sobbing, but saying not a word, then putting her gently aside, he left the room.

To her great surprise her dinner of bread and milk was presently bought up by Agnes, who set it down and went out without exchanging a word with her.

The same thing occurred at suppertime.

Lulu began to be filled with curiosity not unmingled with apprehension, but was too proud to question the girl.

All through the afternoon and evening, her thoughts dwelt much upon what her father had said to her, and the words and tender tones of his prayer rang in her ears and melted her heart. Besides, she had become thoroughly convinced that what he said he would do, so that there was no hope of release until won by obedience.

She was disappointed that he did not come with her supper nor afterward, for she had almost resolved to submit. She cried herself to sleep that night, feeling such a love for her father as she had never known before, and an intense longing for his kiss of forgiveness.

She became not willing only, but eager to do his bidding that she might receive it.

In the morning she dressed herself with neatness and care and impatiently awaited his coming. She was sure it must be long past the usual hour when at last the door opened and Violet came in with the tray of bread and milk.

She set it down and turned to the little girl, who stood gazing at her in silent surprise.

"Lulu, dear, your father is very ill," she said in tones quivering with emotion, and then the child noticed that there were traces of tears about her eyes and on her cheeks. "He was in terrible pain all night, and is very little better this morning," she went on. "Oh, Lulu, I had a dear, dear father once, and he was taken ill very much as yours has been and — died in a few days. Oh, how I loved him! And while he lived I thought I was a good daughter to him, for I don't remember ever being willfully disobedient. But after he was gone my heart reproached me with having neglected opportunities to give him pleasure, and not having always obeyed quite so promptly and cheerfully as I might, and I would have given worlds to go back and be and do as I ought."

She ended with a burst of tears, covering her face with her hands and sobbing, "Oh, papa, papa! Oh, my husband, my dear, dear husband!"

"Oh, Mamma Vi! I will ask your pardon — I do! Won't you please forgive me for being so very, very naughty and impertinent? When you had been so good and kind to me, too," sobbed Lulu, dropping on her knees at Violet's feet.

"I do with all my heart," Violet said, lifting her up and kissing her. "And shall we not always love each other for your dear father's sake?"

"Oh, yes, yes, indeed! I do love you! I don't know

what made me be so wicked and stubborn. Mayn't I go to papa and tell him how sorry I am, and ask him to forgive me, too?"

"Yes, dear, come; perhaps it may help him to grow better, for I know he has grieved very much over this," Vi said, taking the child's hand and leading her into the room where the captain lay.

As he saw them come in thus his eye brightened in spite of the severe pain he was enduring.

With one bound, Lulu was at his side, sobbing, "Papa, papa! I'm so sorry for all my badness, and all your pain. Please, please forgive me. I've done it — asked Mamma Vi's pardon, and — and I'll never talk so to her again, nor ever disobey you anymore."

"I hope not, my darling," he said, drawing her down to give her a tender fatherly kiss of forgiveness. "I am rejoiced that you have given up you rebellion so that now I can love and cuddle you to my heart's content — if God spares me to get up from this bed of pain. I do forgive you gladly, dear daughter."

For several days the captain was very ill, but the best medical advice was at hand, the best of nursing was given him by Elsie and Violet, assisted by Mr. and Mrs. Dinsmore and others, and, by the blessing of Providence, upon these means he recovered.

Lulu seemed very unhappy and remorseful until it was quite certain that he would get well. She took little interest in any kind of recreation, and was often found hovering about the door of his room, eager to learn how he was and if possible gain admission to his presence, or permission to do something for his relief.

She was a changed child from that time, perfectly respectful, obedient, and affectionate toward both her father and Violet.

When the captain had once begun to mend, the improvement was very rapid, and he was soon able to share in the drives and other recreations of their party.

During his illness Grandma Elsie had been very kind to his children, acting a mother's part by them, attending to their wants, comforting and encouraging them with hope of his recovery, and they had grown very fond of her.

At first Lulu shrank from all her new mamma's relatives, and even from Max and Gracie, ashamed of her misconduct and expecting to receive unpleasant reminders of it.

But she met with nothing of the kind, except that Max, when she first came downstairs, said, "It does seem strange, Lulu, that when so many men have to obey papa the instant he speaks, his own little girl should stand out so long and stubbornly against his authority." And Gracie, with her arms about her sister's neck sobbed, "Oh, Lu, how could you make dear papa so sorry for so many days?"

"Was he so sorry?" sobbed Lulu.

"Yes, indeed. Sometimes he hardly ate anything, and looked so sad that the tears came in my eyes and in Mamma Vi's too."

"Oh, I hope that wasn't what made him sick!" cried Lulu, the tears streaming down her face. "I'll never, never behave so to him again."

Lulu was still more remorseful as time went on and everybody was so kind to her, seeming never to remember her naughtiness and disgrace, but giving her a share in all the pleasures devised for themselves which were suitable to her age.

She was especially touched and subdued by the interest Violet took in seeing her provided with new dresses made and trimmed in the fashion (which, to her extreme vexation, Mrs. Scrimp had always disregarded), and with many other pretty things.

When she thanked her new mamma, she was told, "Your father pays for them all, dear."

Then she went to him with tears in her eyes, and putting her arms round his neck, thanked him for all his goodness, confessing that she did not deserve it.

"You are very welcome, nevertheless, daughter," he said, "and all I ask in return is that you will be good and obedient."

Vi wished to return to Lulu the pink coral ornaments, but that he would not allow.

It was a great disappointment to Lulu, for she admired them extremely, but she showed herself extremely submissive under it.

Chapter XXIII

Max

"Papa," said Max one morning, as they rose from the breakfast table, "I feel as if a long walk would do me good. I'd like to go farther down the beach than I ever have yet."

"Very well, my son, you may go, only keep out of danger and come home in time for dinner," was the indulgent rejoinder, and the lad set off at once.

He presently fell in with two other lads a little older than himself, boarders in one of the near hotels, and casual acquaintances of his. They joined him and the three rambled on together, whistling, talking, and occasionally stooping to pick up a shell, pebble or bit of seaweed or sponge.

At length they reached an inlet that seemed to bar their farther progress. But looking about they spied an old boat stranded by yesterday's tide a little higher up the inlet, and were, of course, instantly seized with a great desire to get her into the water and set sail in her.

"Wouldn't it be jolly fun?" cried Bob Masters, the eldest of the trio. "Come on, boys."

Max was a rather heedless fellow and never stopping to consider right or wrong of the thing, or whether he were running into danger or not, went with the others.

They found the boat, as they thought in fair condition. There were two oars in her, and both Max and John Cox, the other lad, thought they knew pretty well how to use them, while Masters was sure he could steer.

With a good deal of exertion they set the little craft afloat. Then, climbing in they pushed boldly out into deep water and bore down toward the ocean.

Max had thought they were only going to cross to the

farther side of the inlet and continue their walk. But, almost before he knew it, they were out upon the sea, and the boat was rocking upon the waves in a way that seemed to him decidedly alarming.

"Boys," he said, "let's put back as fast as we can. We don't know anything about managing a boat out here, and see how big the waves are?"

"That's because the tide's coming in," laughed Masters, "so if we should upset it'll wash us ashore."

"I don't know," said Max, "I'd rather not risk it. There's the undertow to carry us out again."

"Oh, you're a coward!" sneered Cox.

"I'm not going to turn back yet," said Masters. "So stick to your oar, Raymond, and if the sight of the big waves frightens you, just turn your back to 'em."

At that moment a hail came from a fishing smack not far away. "Halloo! Boys, you'd better put back as fast as you can. That boat's not safe, especially in the hands of such greenhorns as you."

At the same moment a big incoming wave washed over them, carrying away their hats and Max's coat, which he had pulled off when taking the oar.

Masters and Cox were now sufficiently frightened to turn back. They made the attempt at once, but found it far more difficult than they had anticipated. They struggled hard, and several times nearly gave themselves up for lost; but, at last, after many narrow escapes, a huge wave carried them high on to the beach, and left there with barely strength to crawl up out of the way of the next wave.

It was a good while before they were able to do anything but lie panting and gasping on the sand.

Max had not been long gone when Zoe ran into the cottage of the Raymonds, to tell of a plan just set foot on the other house to get up a party to visit some points of interest several miles distant.

They were to go in carriages, take a lunch with them, and not return till late in the afternoon, when all would dine together at Mrs. Dinsmore's table.

"Mamma is not going," she said, "and offers to take care of Gracie, if the child stays behind. Everyone seems to fear the ride would be too long and wearisome for her."

"Yes, I think so," the captain said, cuddling her, for she was sitting on his knee.

"I'd like to go, papa," she said, looking coaxingly into his face. "I like to go driving, and to sit on your knee."

"And I love to have my baby girl in my arms, and to give her pleasure," he responded, repeating his caresses, "but I should feel very sad to see her made sick."

"Then I'll be good and not ask to go, papa," she said, with a slight sigh, laying her head on his shoulder.

"That's my dear, good little Gracie! You shall have a short drive every day when I can manage it. Perhaps a moonlit drive along the beach tomorrow evening — will that be nice?"

"Oh, ever so nice, dear papa!" she cried, clapping her hands in delight.

"Mamma not going, Zoe?" exclaimed Violet in a tone of disappointment. "That will rob the excursion of half its charm for me. Is she not well?"

"She has a very slight headache, she says, and fears the sun would increase it. Besides, she is so much interested in a book she is reading that she prefers staying at home to finish it. We had hard work to persuade grandpa to go without her, but he has consent at last. Only, I believe because Grandma Rose refused to go without him and mamma insists that she is in no danger of a bad headache if she keeps quiet."

"Yes, grandpa is so fond and careful of her."

"We have two large carriages, so that there is abundant room for everybody," pursued Zoe. "And we hope, Captain, that you will let Max and Lulu go."

"Lulu shall certainly, if she chooses," he said, turning with a kind, fatherly smile to the little girl who stood silently at his side. She was waiting with a wistful, eager look, to hear if she were to be of the party, but ashamed to ask the indulgence because of a vivid remembrance of her late rebellion and disgrace.

"Oh, thank you, papa!" she cried joyously, giving him a hug and kiss. "Mamma Vi, what shall I wear?"

"Your travelling dress will be the most suitable, I think," said Violet.

"Then I'll run and put it on," returned Lulu, hastening away with cheerful alacrity.

"Max shall go too, Captain, shan't he?" queried Zoe, with whom the boy was a great favorite.

"He might if he were here," the father answered, "but unfortunately he has gone off for a long walk and may not be back before dinner time."

"And we must start in a few minutes," remarked Vi. "I am really sorry, for I know Max will regret missing it. Gracie dear, I'm going over to speak to mamma. Shall I take you with me?"

"Yes, if you please, Mamma Vi, when I've kissed my dear papa goodbye."

Having done so, she took her doll in her arm and gave her hand to Violet. She felt a little lonely at the thought of being left behind, but was quite comforted on learning that little Walter Travilla had decided to stay at home and play with her.

The sightseers drove off, and Elsie, having provided the little ones with amusement, gave herself up to the enjoyment of her book and an easy chair set where she could catch the pleasant sea breeze without feeling the sun. Still, she did not forget the children, but now and then laid aside her book for a little while, while she suggested or invented some new game for their entertainment.

So the morning passed quietly and pleasantly.

It was a little past noon when, stepping out on the veranda, she caught sight of a forlorn figure — hatless, coatless and disheveled generally — approaching the other cottage. A second glance told her who it was.

"Max! Can it be you?" she asked. "Why, my poor boy, where have you been? And what has happened to you?"

"Oh, Grandma Elsie!" he said, looking much mortified and ready to cry, "I did hope I'd be able to get into the house without anybody seeing me! Do you know where my father is?"

"Yes, the two families have all gone on an excursion except Gracie, Walter and me. But come in out of the sun," she added, leading the way into the Raymonds' cottage. Max followed her, and won to confidence by her sweet and kindly sympathy, told her the whole story of his morning's adventure.

"Oh, Max, my dear boy! What a narrow escape you've had!" she said, with tears in her eyes. "What a mercy that you are alive to tell the tale! What a terrible, terrible shock it would have been to your father to learn that his only son was drowned! And that while in the act of disobeying him, for you say he bade you not to into danger."

"Yes, Grandma Elsie, and if he finds it out I'll be pretty sure to get a severe flogging. I deserve it, I know; but I don't want to take it. You won't tell on me, will you? Perhaps he'll find out through the loss of the coat and hat, but I hope he won't miss them, as I have several others."

"No, Max, I shall certainly not tell on you. No one shall ever learn from me what you have told me in confidence. But I do hope, my dear boy, that you will not try to deceive your kind, loving father, but will confess all to him as soon as he comes home, and patiently bear whatever punishment he seems fit to inflict. It is the only right and honorable course, Max, and will save you a great deal of suffering from remorse and fear of detection."

"But it will be dreadfully hard to confess!" sighed Max. "I believe I really dread that more than the flogging."

"Yet take courage, my boy, and do it. Do not allow yourself to indulge in moral cowardice, but dare to do right, asking help of God, who is able and willing to give it."

Max made no reply, but sat there before her, looking very guilty and miserable.

"You must be hungry," she said presently, "and it is not easy to be brave and strong on an empty stomach. Suppose you go to your room and make yourself neat, then come into the other house and join me and the little folks in a nice luncheon."

The proposal was accepted with thankfulness.

Max looked several degrees less miserable after satisfying his appetite, yet all the afternoon he seemed restless and unhappy.

Elsie said little to him, but many times silently lifted up her heart on his behalf, asking that he might have strength given him to do the duty he felt to be so difficult and painful.

As the time drew near when the sightseers might be expected to return, he slipped away out of her sight.

Presently the carriage drove up and deposited their passengers. Max stood waiting on the veranda, his heart beating very fast and loud, as his father, Violet and Lulu came up the path that led from the garden gate.

All three greeted him affectionately, expressing their regret that he had missed the pleasure of the excursion. Then, Vi and Lulu passed into the house and on upstairs.

The captain was about to follow when Max, stepping close to his side, said, with a slight tremble in his voice, "Papa, I — want to speak to you."

"Very well, my son, say on," answered the captain, stopping and turning toward him.

"It's something I want to tell you, sir," and Max hung his head, his cheeks flushing hotly.

His father gave him a searching look, took his hand, and led him into the parlor.

"Don't be afraid of your father, Max," he said kindly, "Why should you?"

"Because I've been a bad boy, sir, deserving of a flogging, and expect you to give it to me," Max burst out desperately.

"Tell me all about it, my son," the captain said in a moved tone, "and tell it here," seating himself and drawing the boy to his knee. "Perhaps it will be easier."

"Oh, yes, papa, because it makes me know you love me even if I am bad; but it makes me more ashamed and sorry for having disobeyed you," sobbed Max, no longer able to refrain from tears as he felt the affectionate clasp of his father's enfolding arm.

"Then it has a right effect. My boy, I think if you knew how much I love you, you would never disobey. It will be a sore trial to me, as well as to you, if I find it my duty to inflict any severe punishment upon you. But let me hear your story."

Max told it in broken accents, for he was full of remorse for having behaved so ill to so kind a parent.

When he had finished there was a moment of silence. It was the captain who broke it.

"My boy," he said, with emotion, "It was a really wonderful escape, and we must thank God for it. If you had been drowned, Max, do you know that it would have gone near to breaking your father's heart? To lose my first born, my only son, and in the very act of disobedience — oh, how terrible!"

"Papa, I didn't, I really didn't think about its being disobedience when I got into the boat, because it didn't seem dangerous till we were fairly out among the waves."

"Do you think I ought to excuse you on that account?"

"No, sir. You've reproved me so often for not thinking, and for not being careful to obey your orders. And I know I deserve a flogging. But, oh, papa, please don't let Mamma Vi know about it, or anybody else. Can't you take me upstairs here when they are all in the other house?"

"I shall not use corporal punishment this time, Max," the captain said, in a moved tone, pressing the boy closer to his side. "I shall try free forgiveness, for I think you are truly sorry. And then you have made so frank and full a confession of wrong doing that I might perhaps never have discovered in any other way."

"Oh, papa, how good you are to me! I don't think I can ever be so mean and ungrateful as to disobey you again," exclaimed Max, feelingly. "But I don't deserve to be praised, or let off from punishment, for I shouldn't have done it if Grandma Elsie hadn't talked to me about the duty of it, and persuaded me to take courage to do it because it was right."

"Bless her for it! The dear, good woman!" the captain said, with earnest gratitude. "But I think, Max, you do deserve commendation for taking her advice. I have something more to say to you, my son, but not now, for the call to dinner will come directly and I must go and prepare for it."

There was a hearty embrace between them, and they separated. The captain went to his room to get ready for dinner and Max to the other house, where he soon managed to let Grandma Elsie into the secret of his confession and its happy result, thanking her with tears in his eyes for her kind, wise advice.

Elsie rejoiced with and for him, telling him he had made her heart glad and that she hoped he would always have courage to do right.

As Max prepared for bed that night he was wondering to himself what more his father had to say to him, when he heard the captain's steps on the stairs, and the next moment he came in.

Max started a little apprehensively. Could it be that his father had changed his mind and was about to give him the dreaded flogging after all?

But with one glance up into the grave yet kindly face looking down at him, all his fear vanished. He drew a long breath of relief.

"My boy," the captain said, laying his hand on Max's shoulder, "I told you I had something more to say to you, and I have come to say it now. You are 'my first born, my might and the beginning of my strength.' Never until you are a father yourself can you know or understand the tide of love, joy, and thankfulness that swept over me at the news of your birth. Nor do you know how often, on land and on sea, in storm and in calm, my thoughts dwell with deep anxiety upon the future of my son — not only for time, Max, but for eternity."

The captain paused for a moment, his emotions

seemingly too big for utterance, and Max, throwing his arms around his neck, hid his face on his shoulder.

"Papa," he sobbed, "I didn't know you loved me so much! Oh, I wish I'd always been a good boy!"

The captain sat down and drew him to his knee.

"My dear son," he said, "I have no doubt that you are sorry for every act of disobedience toward me, and I fully and freely forgive them all; but what I want you to consider now is your sinfulness toward God, and your need of forgiveness from Him. You are old enough to be a Christian now, Max, and it is what I desire for you more than anything else. Think what blessedness to be made a child of God, an heir of glory! To have Jesus, the sinner's Friend for your own Savior, your sins all washed away in His precious blood, His righteousness put upon you."

"Papa, I don't know how."

" 'Believe on the Lord Jesus Christ and thou shalt be saved,' the Bible says. It tells us that we have all broken God's holy law, that we all deserve His wrath and curse forever, and cannot be saved by anything that we can do or suffer; but that 'God so loved the world that He gave His only begotten Son, that whosoever believeth in Him should not perish but have everlasting life.' He offers this salvation to us as His free gift, and so we are able to take it, for we can have it no other way. Go to God, my son, just as you have come to me, with confession of your sins and acknowledging that you deserve only punishment; but pleading for pardon through the blood and merits of Jesus Christ. Accept the salvation offered you by the Lord Jesus, giving yourself to Him to be His, His only forever. 'Him hath God exalted with His right hand to be a Prince and a Savior, to give repentance to Israel and remission of sins,' and He will give them to you if you ask for them with all your heart. He says, 'Him that cometh to me, I will in no wise cast out.' My son, my dear son, will not you come now? God's time is always now, and only the present is ours."

"Papa, I will try. I am sorry for my sins against God, and I do want to belong to Him. Papa, won't you pray for me?"

They knelt down together, and with his son's hand in his, the captain poured out a fervent prayer on the boy's behalf, of confession and entreaty for pardon and acceptance in the name and for the sake of Him "who was delivered for our offences, and was raised again for our justification."

Then, with a silent, tender embrace he left him.

CHAPTER XXIV

Home again, home again, from a foreign shore,
And oh it fills my soul with joy
to see my friends once more.

THE REST OF THE SUMMER and early fall passed
delightfully to the sojourners by the sea. The happiness
of the captain and Violet was somewhat marred by the
knowledge that soon they must part for a season of
greater or less duration — he to be exposed to all the
dangers of the treacherous deep.

But they did not indulge in repining or lose the
enjoyment of the present in vexing thoughts concerning
the probable trials of the future.

It was necessary, however, to give it some consideration,
and make arrangements in regard to his children.

Thinking of the guidance and control they all needed,
the temper and stubbornness of Lulu had shown, the
watchful care requisite for Gracie in her feeble state, he
hesitated to ask Mrs. Dinsmore and Elsie if they still felt
inclined to undertake the charge of them.

But to his great relief and gratitude, those kind
friends did not wait for him to broach the subject, but
renewed their offer, saying they had become much
attached to the children, and desired more than ever to
give them a happy home with themselves. All was, of
course, upon the conditions formerly stated, namely,
that he would delegate his authority to them during his
absence, and give the children distinctly to understand
that he had done so.

These conditions the captain gladly accepted. He told
the children all about the arrangement he had made for
them, and in the presence of the whole family, bade them

obey Mr. and Mrs. Dinsmore, Grandma Elsie and Mamma Vi as they would obey himself.

"One master and three mistresses!" Edward remarked lightly. "Are you not imposing rather hard conditions, Captain?"

"No, I think not, Ned, for I am satisfied that their commands will never conflict. But, should they do so, Mr. Dinsmore, as patriarch of the whole tribe, is of course the highest authority."

It had been decided that Harold and Herbert should now enter college. The others, on being left by the captain, would all return to Ion and spend the winter there or at Viamede. Edward would take charge of the Ion plantation, his grandfather giving him some slight supervision at the start.

This arrangement would leave Mr. Dinsmore almost without employment, and , as he liked to be busy, he said he would gladly act the part of tutor to Max, and also hear some of the recitations of Rosie and Lulu. Grandma Elsie and Mamma Vi would for the present undertake the rest of the work of educating the girls and little Walter.

Their plans settled, they gave themselves up to quiet enjoyment of each other's company while Captain Raymond waited for orders.

Early in October there came a great and joyful surprise. A train had steamed into the neighboring depot a few moments before, but as they were not looking for any addition to their party, no one had taken particular note of the fact.

But a carriage came driving from that direction, and drew up before the gate of Mr. Dinsmore's cottage, where the whole family was gathered.

A gentleman hastily alighted, handed out a lady. A servant woman followed — having first handed him an odd-looking, rather large bundle, which he received with care — then turned to collect packages and parcels, while the other two hurried to the house, the lady a little in advance.

"Elsie!" was the simultaneous exclamation of many

voices in varied tones of astonishment and delight, and the next instant there was a wonderful confusion of greetings and embraces mingled with tears of joy and thankfulness.

Lester and his wife had been heard from frequently during the past months, their letters always cheerful and full of bright hopes and anticipations, but containing no hint of any intention of returning to America before the coming spring.

As they afterward explained, it had been a very sudden resolve, caused by a severe fit of homesickness, and there really was no time to write.

Lester shared the joyous welcome given to Elsie; the servant woman having relieved him of his bundle, of which, in their joyous excitement, no one had taken particular notice.

Only waiting, a trifle impatiently, till the greetings and introductions were over, Elsie Leland took it from her, and with a proud, happy, yet tearful smile laid it — a lovely sleeping babe — in her mother's arms.

"Our boy, mother dear. We have named him for his grandpa — Edward Travilla."

Elsie Travilla folded the child to her heart, kissed it softly, tenderly, the great silent tears rolling down her cheeks.

"Ah, could he but have seen it! Our first grandchild," she sighed.

Then, wiping away her tears, and sending a glance of mingled joy and maternal pride around the little circle, she folded the babe still closer, saying, with an arch, sweet smile, "Ah, no one now can deny that I am in very truth Grandma Elsie!"

The End